When you need a job done, you need a woman.

Tia—codename Cat—knows all about loss. Orphaned at a young age, she's made it through a series of foster homes, with one single aim in sight. Joining the Australian army. Now an accomplished sniper with the *Alathea Rangers*—an all-woman team, begun in Greece and now based in America—covert operations team, she's found where she belongs. Or has she?

When she's sent to retrieve the child of an Australian diplomat, she drops into Zabuti—an unstable African country — with no illusions about her importance in the greater scheme of things.

When Cal sees Cat's landing, he's unsure about the man. His misgivings are even more grave when he realises Cat's female. Can this slight woman do the job? He's supposed to be her in-country guide, but though he packs a gun and is a CIA operative, he can't keep them safe.

The stakes are raised on the wild race across Zabuti, and nothing can prepare him for what's to come, including the passion that rises between them.

In the end, nothing is certain, including their survival.

TIA'S REDEMPTION

IMOGENE NIX

ALATHEA RANGERS

The *Alathea Rangers* were formed by Cara Xenopoulos—a half American half Greek national— pulling together the best and the brightest warriors seeking new challenges.

When Cara's brother Xander died on a mission off the coast of Libya, Cara was a member of the Greek Army, but the mission wasn't just covert, it represented the dark underbelly of military services. Cara was disgusted and withdrew from the army and later formed the original team, many of whom have moved on, having come to terms with the darkness they've seen and the deeds they've done.

With the assistance of an independently wealthy backer, Cara moved her team to America and now runs the *Alathea Rangers*, personally authorising team members missions.

They exist outside the government, for honour and for the protection of society and to save the weak.

Tia's Redemption

Cover Art by Jocelyn Dex - Dexpress Covers

https://dexpresscovers.com

Editing by Hot Tree Editing

EBook ISBN 978-1-922369-55-0

PROLOGUE

Tia dragged herself from the pool, chest heaving and arms shaking. "Fifty fucking laps. I did it." Once on the concrete, she slumped, ignoring the scratch and the wet patch.

"Mum'll have a cow because you're swearing again," called Vanessa, her much younger foster sister.

Tia closed her eyes. *One-one hundred, two-one hundred.* It wasn't that Vanessa was difficult. She was just young and still very innocent.

Tia knew the house rules, so there wasn't any way she could claim ignorance after seventeen and a half months.

Hell, she'd been through a myriad of similar arguments already— at least four other times. But this was her last foster care placement. Only three weeks left of school to go; then she'd be gone and on her own. *Freedom never felt sweeter,* she silently acknowledged. The letter she'd been waiting for arrived yesterday, confirming she'd made it through the rigorous army intake process.

"Sorry," she muttered, knowing full well if she didn't, Vanessa would tell, and all Tia wanted now was an easy transition out of care. She pushed up from the ground. "We should go home."

Vanessa's eyes drew together. "What about your run?"

Tia couldn't restrain the laugh. "I did that while you were still asleep, kiddo. This morning. Five kilometres isn't a lot in the grand scheme of things, you know." And it wasn't when you only slept five to six hours a night. Less when memories haunted her.

Even now, after years of therapy, they still cropped up, stressed her like sitting final exams or waiting for a letter that would ultimately allow her to start her life.

Tia stepped over to her bag where it sat on the polished aluminium seating and slid into the coverall she'd stashed at the top. Then she tugged the rope handles of the canvas bag over her shoulder.

Tia stared at the younger girl, hoping she'd wordlessly gather her swim bag. At eleven, Vanessa was cute but pushy, with curling blonde hair and sweet blue eyes to fit the round face and Cupid's bow lips. *When she grows up, the boys will be lining up.*

The only natural child of her foster carer, Vanessa had seen kids come and go and handled it like a pro. Not that Tia was concerned. She treated her the same way she treated her classmates. Did what she had to but nothing more. Encouraging any kind of lasting relationship wasn't on Tia's radar.

"Mummy said you got a letter from the army. When are you leaving?"

It took Tia every ounce of willpower not to retort "as soon as possible" and instead answered, "Three weeks, kiddo."

"But you'll come back and see us, right? Like some of the others?" Vanessa didn't whine so much as attack the words as a fact. That set Tia's teeth on edge.

"Maybe," she muttered as she unlocked the aging Toyota she'd bought with money given by the executors of her parents' will. There was more, but she kept it stashed for the proverbial "rainy day" she was sure would come at some point. "Come on. Get in and buckle up. You've got homework, and I need to get my dress out for tonight."

The leaver's dinner was one small highlight in the lead-up to getting out of this central Queensland town that she wouldn't forego. It was a rite of passage. She'd even sprung for her hair to be styled this afternoon and her make-up to be applied.

ONE

Several Years Later

Somewhere in Western Zabuti, Africa

Sarah whimpered in the near dark.

She hated it. The scuttling of creatures and the horrible smelly rag they'd shoved in her mouth. Her belly hurt with hunger, and she really had to go to the toilet. Sarah squirmed again, trying to hold on a little longer.

All she wanted was to go home to her daddy. Tears burned in her eyes, and she blinked. It didn't make them go away.

The hut at least meant she was out of the sun, Sarah thought, glancing up to the roof. It was still day. She knew because sunbeams covered bits of the ground. If only she could scoot over, but they'd tied her tight to this pole, and it itched.

The door opened, and a woman stepped in. Came close. "You need a toilet. Eat and drink."

The bucket didn't look like any toilet she'd ever used, but the pain from holding on meant she had to accept assistance from the woman who loomed over her. She wasn't dark-skinned like the people in the uniforms who'd taken her. She was older and white, her hair streaked with grey through the black strands, and her breath stank. Sarah edged away because it upset her tummy.

When she'd finished, the woman dragged the cloth from her mouth, and she sipped cautiously at the water. It didn't taste great, but Sarah was thirsty. At least they'd given her a straw. When the water was gone, the woman fed her bits of bread before shoving the cloth back into her mouth.

"Gleg meh gaah," Sarah yelled, but the woman smiled.

"Soon, little buttercup. You're still useful to us." Then the woman retreated, and the door shut, leaving Sarah alone again.

She bowed her head and cried.

Looking down at the folder Cara had shoved into her hands, Tia wondered what the latest mission would entail.

The familiar fizz of excitement hummed through her veins at the thought of what might lie ahead. It wasn't so much that Tia enjoyed the danger, just that she was bloody good at her job.

"Where and what?" She glanced up, noting how Cara's gaze ran over her. She knew what the other woman saw. A fair and delicate face, totally at odds with the person she'd become over the years—dark eyes with a tiny hint of an almond shape, a leftover from some long-forgotten antecedent. A woman not really tall, but neither could she be considered tiny. A package that hid who and what she really was: a trained assassin and sniper when Alathea Rangers required it.

"It's an extraction. But we'll be needing your sniper skills and cunning." Cara frowned as she explained.

Tia shook her head. "I don't usually do extractions, Cara. You know that. One of the others...." They really weren't her forte, though she'd been on enough such missions and helped organize her part in the role to know the ropes.

"This one is sensitive, Tia. You've been particularly chosen because you're Australian." Cara inhaled deeply, and for a moment, apprehension filled Tia, but she shrugged it off.

"Why?"

Cara's eyes turned hard. "The young daughter of an Australian diplomat was abducted from embassy grounds in Zabuti. They don't want to send in national forces because that would undermine some very fragile negotiations they're involved in, but the kid is in serious danger from the militia. There's even talk of connections to Al-Qaeda. You know what that means."

Tia's stomach dropped hard. "Why the kid, though? Why not the father?"

"The kid's seven, Tia, and we think it's a leverage kind of situation. She was snatched from the embassy where she'd been playing on the grounds and should have been safe."

Tia frowned. Kids. She wasn't so great with them. "And?"

"Her father thinks she'd be leery of anyone not from Australia, so we're sending you in. She's more likely to trust you when you speak. Your task is to find her, extract her to awaiting transport. You'll have a contact within the American embassy, but you can't take her back there because they'll simply try again. We believe she's still alive, though we can't confirm that. Realistically, if they get their hands on her after successful extraction, that won't be the case again." Cara steepled her fingers, pinning Tia with cold, dead eyes.

Tia had seen enough of Cara in action to know the woman was just as deadly with and without a weapon. "And I'm the only Aussie on the team."

Cara nodded as if reading her thoughts. "You're going to have to travel overland through the desert, then cross the border. On foot, Tia. With the kid in tow. It'll be rough, but you'll meet up with a contact, and they'll escort you across the border."

Tia's nostrils flared, and heat shot through her. "I don't need a bodyguard, Cara."

The other woman smiled, but it was slight and barely reached her eyes. "No, you don't. But the kid will. You can't be awake 24/7, Tia, and to be frank, we have so little knowledge of this locality, unlike our contact. This case could have serious political ramifications, so you're going to have to accept a partner." Cara shoved the file again. "Read it. Memorize the facts and information. Learn the kid's face, then return the file."

Tia looked down at the manila folder in her hand. It wasn't very thick, and that alone gave her pause. They usually had more information to even begin the planning process.

"Where you're going, there can't be any paperwork or mistakes because she could die. The kid is counting on you for her survival. It's going to be hell out there."

"Sure," Tia answered and settled down at the desk, flipping the front cover open as Cara left her alone.

Tia scoured the kid's face. The bright blue eyes, the small dimple in her still chubby cheeks. No earrings, but a little mole on her left cheek. An identifying feature she could rely on. She learned the girl —Sarah—was the only child of a senior Aussie diplomat. His wife had died two years previously from cancer, and as the stay had been expected to be prolonged, he'd chosen to bring his daughter with him. "Big mistake." Tia shook her head.

Reading on, she gleaned he was there to help the tiny African country throw off the military administration chains resulting from a coup that had succeeded twenty years before.

"I remember that. Zabuti was just emerging, and the situation was violent," she muttered to herself. Many deaths occurred during the revolt. The military had hung on for grim death until nearly fifteen years later. Even now, democracy emerged battered and confused. The fledgling government would fail without western countries' support, she knew, having seen the regular updates on the news channels.

Tia read the report on the security on the embassy grounds. Two guards at the main entrance and only three patrolling at any given time. The lax measures came about because the externally sourced guards had become complacent.

Her mind whirred as she tapped the computer screen to her left. It gave them access to most any database in the world, and not for the first time, Tia silently thanked Sharon, their resident tech-head, for her magic ability with the machines that bedevilled Tia.

"I can barely program my coffee machine," she groused even as she checked the detailed maps, looking for the best possible location for a drop zone, and formulated her entry into Zabuti. Everywhere she looked, there appeared to be desert, but here and there, she noted small villages and townships. "I'll need to steer clear of any populated areas." It would be rough, but she needed to get in fast, set up a meet, and then get on with the mission at hand. "There's only one way, Tia."

Her favourite tried-and-true measure would be employed for insertion.

Finally satisfied, Tia rose and walked to the in-tray by the door, slid the file on top of the pile, and then opened the door. "Cara? I'm going to grab supplies before heading out. I should be ready to go by 1900 hours. Scare up transport for me, would you? I'll also need some papers for the kid and me, courtesy of our good friend Sharon. I'll be back in an hour and will fill you in on my plan then."

Tia settled herself at the table and drank her coffee while waiting for Cara to drop opposite her. "So, all ready?" Cara asked.

Scrunching up her face, Tia nodded. "Yeah. I've got my stuff together and requisitioned the weapons. All I need is a map. The rest? It's all up here." She tapped the side of her head. "Zabuti. Population 1.1 million approximately. A small country sitting on the edge of the Kalahari—specifically the Kalahari Basin. Neighbours include Namibia, Angola, and Botswana. Political conditions are unstable due to the government moving to a democratic electoral system post–militia coup some twenty years ago. Languages spoken include Buntu, English, and a range of other local dialects."

"You've been busy," Cara murmured.

"Thank heavens for my near eidetic memory," Tia added drily.

"When will you be ready?"

She eyed Cara, wondering not for the first time what made this woman really tick. She was beautiful, accomplished, and yet here she was running a secret pseudo-government-sanctioned specialist team. She knew the basics, but what made her Cara—the intrinsic values the woman held—were hidden well below the surface. If planning was her thing, why did she expect the other team members to make so many arrangements for themselves? Then she shrugged, pushing away the questions. "I need to finish the requisitioning, but barring complications, including accessing documentation, I should be on track for that 1900 hours departure."

"I'll organize the plane, then. You want to fly into—"

"Not straight into Zabuti." She'd considered this while completing her personal tasks away from headquarters, as she usually did. "Ghanzi in Botswana would be best based on location, but it's a hole in the wall. No fuel, and I'd stick out like a sore thumb. South Africa may be a better option if you can swing me a ride. Get me a chopper or similar. I'll helo out and stay off the radar."

"You're mad," Cara muttered, and Tia smiled.

"Perhaps, but you know my motto. Go big or go home."

When Cara left, Tia turned to her kit bag. Already stuffed with survival ration packs, ammunition, and her favourite tools of the trade, she was nearly ready. All that was left to add was the documents she'd requested from Sarah.

Tia knew the risks. Accepted them as part of her life—and potential death. She'd long since set up a trust with a beneficiary. No matter how she tried to ignore the person she'd leave everything to, Vanessa kept trying to make contact. Like the letter in her back pocket. It irked her that she couldn't ignore it, so in silence, with nothing more to prepare, she slid it out and opened the envelope.

Vanessa had appealed yet again to her lawyers to find Tia's location. Tia dropped into the seat and sighed. She'd tried to cut all ties with everyone behind her. Vanessa, it appeared, was more determined than the rest. "Just let me die, okay?"

The door opened, and in walked Leonie from the Rangers extraction team. "What's that? You wanna die?"

Tia rolled her eyes. "No. Van sent another letter and is trying to get in touch. The only reason I have the damn lawyers is to sort out the fucking estate my parents left me," she huffed. Those memories were things best kept behind barriers in her mind. "Van found out about them when they sent paperwork to her mother while I was fostered there. She's been hounding them ever since."

"Thought that was all finalized?"

"It is. Sort of. There are a few outstanding things to go, including the sale of the house, but it's nearly done."

Having only taken the best part of twenty years by the time all the cases and litigation were completed, she no longer felt any real connection to that life or the physical reminders. It was as if Tia, the child, had died that day. *In many ways, I guess I did.* The innocent child had certainly passed away on the floor when faced with the reality of losing the scaffolding of her life.

"Ready to head out?" Leonie inclined her head to the large bag on the floor beside Tia.

"Yeah. Nearly. Just waiting on docs, and then I'm off."

"I'm heading for the gym, so I'll see you when you're back," the woman offered, then reached into the refrigerator for cold water before she turned back with a smile. "Good hunting."

The team was tight-knit, like a family, and in many ways, it reminded Tia of her time in the army. That, too, had felt like a family —until it didn't anymore.

Settling in at the table, Tia dug in the side pocket of her pack, withdrew a plastic-covered map of Africa, and looked for a way out of Zabuti. If she were planning the meet with the transport, it would likely be in Livingstone in Zambia. There they would travel to their eventual extraction point.

They could present as mother and daughter—not that Tia had

any real maternal instincts, but it would allow them to hide in plain sight, and she could fake it, right? That route meant approximately ten days at her usual pace, but she'd be carting a kid. If she slowed down to what she considered a crawl—along the lines of half her average speed—she'd make probably about fifteen kilometres in a day. Not great, but it was achievable.

On the flight, she'd consider extra contingencies, options, and so on, because whoever the contact was, she'd have to ensure they agreed to her plan to get the kid out alive.

Her cell buzzed in her pocket, and she pulled it out.

I'm ready. Come get your stuff.

Their resident geek had come through again. Tia had no idea how she managed to get hold of travel documents and so on, but somehow, they were always acceptable when scrutinized.

She stood and looked down at the kit bag. "Wait here," she told it and smiled at her silliness. The bag wouldn't go anywhere without her, but it was a habit forged in the forces.

TWO

Callum Gallagher shaded his eyes as he waited for the entourage to stop. The black car, not a Taurus like they'd use back home but an anonymous Toyota, pulled up before him. The engine idled, and taking the opportunity to glance one last time over his shoulder, checking he wasn't being followed, he ambled forward.

The door opened, and he slid smoothly inside the interior.

"Mr. Gallagher?" The forty-something man with rumpled hair and deep-set bloodshot eyes leaned forward. "You're—"

"Not here," he said to the man. "Drive to the coffee shop as if this is a social outing," he told the driver.

The car slid forward, and Cal, as he was usually known, watched for a moment, searching for a tail. Satisfied there was none, he addressed the man waiting beside him. "Now, we've got someone inbound. They come recommended. The less you know, the better, but they're good. An Australian, as you suggested."

The man bobbed his head up and down. "Sarah?"

"Our intelligence says she's okay for the moment. The inbound operative has field medical training if it's required."

The man shook, and tears ran down his cheeks. "She's too young. I shouldn't have brought her, but the security team assured me—"

Cal grimaced. The so-called security team wasn't worth even naming. They'd not just been ineffectual, but they'd ignored all the warning signs. The attempted egress the night before, the tailing of vehicles.

The militia had been building up to something for weeks, and the security team hadn't shown any awareness of what was going on. Cal's gut clenched, aware that saying so right now would be counterproductive. Instead, he shared only the tip of his scathing assessment.

"Your security team has more holes than swiss cheese, frankly. I've done a little digging, and there's someone inside." Thank God his countrymen had taken over this aspect of the diplomat's safety. "They've got ties to the militia, and it's how they knew who was their best leverage and how."

The man sweated and mopped his brow, though the temperature wasn't really all that unpleasant. Cal felt a modicum of sympathy for the man. He knew the diplomat was a widower, which meant he needed to bring his little girl with him, but Zabuti wasn't safe—for anyone.

Sure, it had some of the trappings of civilization, with coffee shops and markets, such as they were, but there was a seething underbelly of vice, hatred, and murder. He just hoped the agency that sent the operative, code-named Cat, was as good as their word.

"Okay." The man mopped his brow again. "When she gets back here—"

"She won't be. We'll repatriate her to Australia. Get me some details of a family who she can meet with until you're able to—"

"No!" The word erupted from the diplomat's mouth. "My daughter will return to me." Now he wheezed, and for a moment, Cal wondered if the man was about to have a heart attack.

"It's not safe, sir. Consider for a moment this scenario." He cupped his hands. "You get her back to the embassy. Safe and sound. The operative does their job, but then the militia gets their hands on your daughter again. They've already done this once. Next time, she won't be so lucky. The operative will be gone, on a plane to wherever. Even if we could recall him, the identity of this person is compromised." In front of the car, Cal could see the coffee shop. Time to end the discussion. "This won't work any other way. Yes or no?"

The man wrung his hands. "I'll... I'll get some details together. I'll email—I will come. Just contact me when the job is done."

"I'll send someone to collect them from you, sir. Just in case."

The car slid to a stop, and he released the door, which swung wide. "Sure I can't get you a cup of something?" He spoke clearly, in case someone was listening or watching.

The man shook his head, eyes wide open at the subterfuge.

"Okay. Thanks for the lift," he called and headed into the shop, but not before he noted a man in a jacket. The way he straightened up alerted Cal. *Militia for sure.* He didn't really want a coffee, but as thin as the story was, he'd have to follow through or he'd trigger some kind of panic. That would put little Sarah in greater jeopardy.

Once inside, he ordered a Turkish coffee and settled into a seat against the back of the dining area in an almost hidden location, watching the passers-by and noting the man who followed him into the shop.

Beneath his black hoodie, black eyes glittered and searched.

Cal shrank back into his seat against the wall. At least the building was dark. The man ordered a drink, loitering by the door until a cup was pressed into his hands. With no reason to remain, the man pushed off, and Cal released a breath. His own coffee arrived, thanks to a woman serving, and he sipped, letting the rich aroma wrap around him while he considered the situation.

THE FLIGHTS TO JOHANNESBURG FELT MONOTONOUS. THE FIRST leg to Brazil took ten hours, but then the pilot had to take a mandatory break, so they stayed overnight, electing to remain with the plane. It was comfortable enough, but even a Gulfstream G650 had limitations. Their pilot, Jason, and his co-pilot, Garrett, slept loudly. Tia, meanwhile, had remained alert. She could rest once she was sure of her planning.

At least she could keep her weapons out of sight, and they refuelled quickly enough as soon as they were able to get them back into the sky for the final eleven-and-a-half-hour flight into Joburg.

Garrett entered the main cabin. "Tia, I've got a private call for you incoming."

She nodded and reached out to grab the receiver. "Hey, Cara?"

"Tia, we've got someone meeting you on the ground in Johannesburg. David Mac's an ex-SEAL, and he'll have your ride waiting. He's managed to scare up a chute and the safety gear you requested, but he says no flight today. There's instability in the atmosphere over Zabuti, and he won't risk his team."

"Shit!" She rubbed her brow. "Right, tell him I need information when we touch down. A briefing on the terrain, what he knows about Zabuti, and the political climate at this time. What on-the-ground knowledge he has will be useful." It wasn't that she was unaware of what she was flying into, but the more intel, the better. If something had blown up overnight that she'd missed—she'd seen that before—it could be fatal to her or the kid.

"Sure. As for your contact, they've agreed to meet on the edge of the Selinda Game Reserve. They've got the GPS coordinates and will meet you there tomorrow. Though they did request that I inform 'The Cat' that hunting is frowned upon."

Tia sighed. "Well, maybe you should inform them I'm not hunting animals."

Without another word, she reached for her map. The locations and information she'd given Cara still looked right. Tia had spent too many years staying alive by trusting her instincts, and they screamed that she'd made the suitable arrangements.

She made a package of her notes. They would be left on the plane when they landed and forwarded to Cara. All she'd take would be her compass and map, her rucksack and weapons. She just hoped Cara had managed to sort out any issues arising from arriving with protein bars, munitions, and so on. More than once, they'd faced difficulties entering countries fully kitted out. She didn't have time to waste, given her assessment of the situation.

A grunt echoed on the line. "Remember, Tia. No stupid chances. Get the kid and get out of there."

Tia smiled. "Sure thing, boss. Whatever you say." Then she hung up.

THREE

The transfer at Johannesburg was streamlined, and within an hour of leaving her hotel, she'd climbed into the copter waiting near the international airport. They'd taken off and whizzed over the land, headed on a flight path toward Zabuti. She didn't know what David Mac had entered as his flight plan or the excuses and frankly didn't care. That wasn't her problem.

At least Zabuti didn't have an organized air force. She'd taken some time to question the pilot before take-off and heard they'd been mostly disbanded because they'd be loyal to the previous militia government. It was one more task the Aussies would be undertaking after agreements had been reached. To scout and train those loyal to the new government. To assist them in rebuilding their defence force. It would take years, though. It was also one less concern for Tia.

She checked her equipment one last time. The heavy kit bag she'd fastened to her body and the weapons bag was secured against her leg.

The chopper zoomed over the landscape, and looking down, she saw brown, more brown, and still more. Dotted here and there were scattered remnants of bushes, but there was no real rhyme or reason to the layout.

A tap on her shoulder had her looking back. The headgear clicked as the jump instructor said, "Ready? We'll open the door in a moment."

Tia nodded her understanding and handed over the heavy noise-cancelling helmet, swapping it for the jump helmet she'd brought with her.

She waited, knowing the adrenalin buzz would kick in the moment she pushed herself beyond the doors.

The instructor, secured by a line so he didn't fall, opened the side of the copter. Tia stood, shuffled the few inches toward the door, and held on to the loop.

The man gave her a thumbs up, which she returned. The air buffeted her now, frigid at this high altitude.

One deep breath, she reminded herself, then let go of the strap while lunging forward, the weight of her pack speeding up her free fall. For a moment, the wind currents were pulling at her and the coverall she wore over thermals. The fall toward the earth was now silent, and eddying winds caught at her collar and sleeves. Tia flexed her fingers, forcing the blood to flow and nerves to move, more than aware that frostbite at these heights was a valid concern. In her head, she counted off the seconds since she'd exited the chopper.

At approximately sixty seconds, Tia pulled the cord, and a hard tug upward rewarded her. The heavy weight of her kit bag pulled her back toward the earth, and she grunted. She scanned the horizon, all the while correcting her course with the smaller handholds on the chute, so she danced silently during her descent. Below, the air rushed forward, though slower than before, warming now as she reached lower altitudes.

As always, the tranquillity warred with the rush of adrenalin. Tia calculated, again and again, the trajectory and speed. Finally satisfied, though alert, she used the time to clear her mind, allow herself to focus on the landing and the mission ahead.

Just before she hit the ground, she released her kit bag and watched it plummet, then hit the ground with a plume of dust.

She followed it down, her descent more leisurely, her gaze on the vehicle nearby. "Better be my contact," she muttered as she bent her knees, ready for impact with the earth once more.

Her feet touched, and she rolled with the landing, keeping her body loose while her hand hovered over the weapons bag at her side.

It took only seconds to rise and begin divesting herself of the kit, rolling the chute before retrieving her bag where it lay only metres away.

"Damn good jump," a man's voice called.

She turned, and the first sight of her contact was a shock. He was tall, dark-haired, and in his thirties, she guessed. Early to mid, perhaps, with piercing grey eyes. Taking a moment to orient herself and scan him, she kept her helmet on, though she did reach out a hand.

"Cat?" Now she nodded and reached for her helmet, shaking her hair loose as he inhaled sharply. "You're a woman?"

"Strangely, yes. Who are you?"

He shook his head. "I need someone capable."

If Tia had a dollar for every time someone drew the conclusion that because she was female, she couldn't manage an op, she'd be rich. "Well, I'm the operative you got. Name's Cat. Now, what's your name and designation?"

"Uh, Callum Gallagher, but everyone calls me Cal. CIA. With the American embassy." He still appeared surprised and stumbled over his words while Tia grunted.

"Fine, Mr. G-Man, help me collect and stow everything, and we can get started."

He frowned. "Uh, sure."

It's going to be a difficult mission, Tia told herself, then got busy.

Cal waited in the jeep, the engine running while he scanned the horizon. Another glance at his watch told him the contact was due any time now.

Scanning the distance, he strained for any sound of an engine to alert him that Cat had arrived. The distant drone of a motor had him looking up.

A speck of black was growing bigger while whatever kind of copter they'd used continued its drone. Even as he waited, the spark grew larger. "Son of a bitch!" The operative—Cat—was jumping in.

He watched with awe as Cat floated toward the earth, releasing the large kit bag just seconds before he landed. He ambled forward. "Damn good jump," Cal called and watched as Cat turned. He couldn't help but notice the man wasn't very tall, but hey, if he could do the job, who cared?

The man turned and gazed in his direction, though he did extend a hand. Cal took it and shook, surprised at the almost petite size, but the strength of the grip reassured him. Once the hand released his, "Cat?" Cat reached up and removed his—or rather *her* helmet.

He stared. She stared, her eyes dark and with a tiny hint of Asian heritage if the shape was anything to go by. "You're a woman?" He wanted to shake his head to shrug off the surprise.

"Strangely, yes. Who are you?"

He shook his head, unable to stop the motion. "I need someone capable." The words escaped from his mouth unbidden, and he wanted to wince. They wouldn't have sent her if she wasn't capable. She must have been a member of the legendary, if secretive, Alathea Range, an all-female black ops team.

No one had been sure they actually existed. Not until now.

The only aspect about this operative that made sense was the Australian accent.

"Well, I'm the operative you got. Name's Cat. Now, what's your name and designation?"

He cursed internally that he'd allowed surprise to overrun professionalism. "Uh, Callum Gallagher, but everyone calls me Cal. CIA.

With the American embassy." The woman before him was clearly unimpressed, if the grunt she gave was any indication.

"Fine, Mr. G-Man, help me collect and stow everything, and we can get started."

He frowned. "Uh, sure."

"Right. What intel do you have? I need to get moving."

He shook his head again. "I'm going with you."

Her lips, pale pink and soft looking, took on a mulish expression. "I prefer to work alone, but if you're coming with me, you keep up. The kid is my priority. Fall behind, slow me down, and I'll leave you behind. If it's a choice between her and you, she wins. Got it? I give an instruction, and you follow it." Every word was stern, forceful, and it took a second for him to realize she also meant them.

"I'm not exactly unable to keep up," he muttered.

"What's your regime? It might give me a clue as to how fast you can move."

She battered him with her demand, and he shrugged. "I run five miles every day, lift weights, and—"

Cat shook her head. "Uh-huh. Okay, that's everything I need to know." He didn't detect any appreciation in her tone. In fact, he'd almost say her words were derisive. "I need intel and some last-minute supplies. Where can I get water, warm kids' clothes, and a soft hat? Sneakers and socks for the kid."

He stared at her. "Why?"

"Because if I were them, I'd have taken her shoes, put her in light-weight clothing so she'd be unable to survive in the environment."

He grunted, once more surprised at how she thought. "Uh, there's a market nearby. But you'll stand out in that." He pointed to the coveralls she wore.

"Yep. Let's get this stuff to the vehicle, and I'll change out. I've got alternative clothing in my pack."

He reached for the bag and cursed at the weight. Cat snickered, scooped it out of his hold, and unfastened the bulky weapons bag attached to her leg. When she flung the bag over a shoulder, he collected up the chute and ropes and shadowed her to the vehicle. Once there, Tia unfastened the strapping on the bag, then retrieved a pair of long pants and a long-sleeved shirt. As she started to strip before him, he turned away, his face flaming.

Her laugh surprised him. "You're not the first man I've dressed in front of. SASR didn't care if we were male or female."

Cal frowned. "SASR?"

"Special Air Service Regiment. Australia."

He heard movement and racked his brain, trying to remember what little he knew about that branch of the Aussie army. He guessed they must be like SEALS, but she didn't look like any combat-type personnel he'd had anything to do with.

"You can turn around now."

He did, and his gaze raked over her. Her pants were old-fashioned, a muddy shade akin to khaki mixed with red dust, the fly a button-down variety, and her boots swallowed the legs' hem. Hair pulled back tight against her scalp, though he could still note the glossy strands. On her hands, she wore gloves, fingerless and also in that dull rust colour, and he wondered, not for the first time, if she'd chosen the shade so she'd disappear against the sand of the desert basin.

"Can we get moving now?" He heard the derision in her tones and fought off the blush of embarrassment. "I want to be on the road before nightfall. I don't know the area, and the sooner we're close to the camp, the sooner I can begin my mission." Her voice was lilting, and he wondered how she'd come to this profession.

"Sure." They jumped into the car, and he noticed a canteen in her hands. "Thirsty?"

"No. Just hydrating before we head out. You should too." She thrust the bottle at him, but he shook his head.

He drove smoothly. The ground might have been rutted and rocky here, but soon they'd be on the highway and past the game reserve entrance. "Why did you pick here? There are elephants and...." He turned to look at her.

"Well, the reality is here we were close to the entrance. It's also not an area where I'd expect to run into the militia, which is key." She shrugged, but Cal got the uncanny feeling she'd taken great care with her choice of the landing site.

He continued to drive. The distances seemed vast to him even after long months here, yet she leaned back, apparently unconcerned.

"What more can you tell me about the situation?"

He inhaled, collecting himself before rattling off the scant information that was pertinent. "The father, Matthew Berding, is a widower. Brought Sarah, his daughter, with him because he didn't feel he could leave her behind. He relied on the security forces the embassy has engaged, but my intel says there's a militia operative inside the team. The position of ambassador for Zabuti hasn't been formalized, but it's generally considered that he's the front runner, already being installed here. I doubt he'll stay once his daughter is recovered." He glanced at the landscape, and with no oncoming vehicles, he turned onto the highway. "He's a career diplomat and working with the Zabuti government during the transitionary period. Setting up procedures and so on so they can run democratic elections in two years. He's been liaising with the head of government along with our ambassador. He personally is what you'd expect from a career state office type. The daughter is seven. Bright and was playing in the gardens, abiding by the rules as far as we can tell, when she was taken. She'd been home-schooling during the time here, and her governess was inside preparing lunch."

"What about the political environment? I know Zabuti is throwing off what's been before, but what do the civilians want? Democracy, or are they being shunted that way but naturally aligned with the militia?"

Cal scratched his head. "Most people are in favour of the change. The militia came in promising freedoms that were curtailed pretty quickly after they assumed their position of power. It's not uncommon to have whole families disappear in the night. Rumours abound of murders and kickbacks." He shrugged as he spied the township he'd earmarked for their purchasing expedition ahead. "People are scared of the power they've wielded. Those who know things aren't talking freely, and if even a quarter of what I've heard is true? I wouldn't either."

He slowed the car on the outskirts of town and watched as she sat upright once more, scanning the environment and the small knots of people gathered around.

"You're CIA, right? So, what do you know that you haven't told me?"

He whipped his head around. "What do you mean?"

"CIA are intelligence gatherers. Embedded around the world and very much in the know. What is it I don't yet know? I'm guessing Sarah is bait to make Berding do what they want, right? What are the chances she's already dead? What other avenues have been exhausted in trying to get her back?"

Cal sighed. *So much for being satisfied with what I've already told her.* "There's a little more. I'll tell you all after we finish here."

He noted how her eyes narrowed, but she didn't say a word as he pulled up to the shop.

"We both go in?"

Cat shook her head. "No. Here's my list. You go in, get what's needed. I'll stay here with my pack," she answered as he parked. It was clear she didn't trust anyone else, so he shrugged and entered the market, the sheet of paper in his hand. Her writing was sparse, with no curls or unnecessary crosses.

He grabbed precisely what she asked for, only adding a single candy bar on a whim—a tracksuit for the girl, sandshoes, and four sets of socks. Cal wondered about that but shrugged. Several bottles of water, a bottle of alcohol—he raised his eyes at that inclusion—and soap. Unscented.

His arms were full when he retreated to the vehicle, noting she was under the back, running her hands along the metal. "Looking for something?"

When she stood up, brushed off her hands and knees, he could almost swear she was smiling. "You have a tracker on the car. We'll need to ditch it before we head out."

Now it was his turn to smile. "No, it's ours. We've started tagging the cars to keep track via GPS of where they're going."

"You still need to get rid of it."

Cal scowled. "What do you mean?"

She knelt, slid her hand under the back, and wrenched. With a pop, the tracker came free, and he wasn't fast enough to stop the stomp of her booted foot on the device. It fizzed, popped, and likely died in that instant, Cal thought.

"Now we can go."

"What? Why did you do that?"

"I'll tell you in the car, Gallagher."

"Cal," he corrected her.

"Sure thing. Whatever floats your boat."

FOUR

"What was that all about?" he demanded once they'd cleared the township.

Tia didn't enjoy acting the arse, but today it was necessary. She had to make sure he understood she was in charge of this operation.

"We don't know who else is on the inside, do we? You've not yet told me everything, but I'm guessing the Aussie contingent has a traitor, right?"

He nodded slowly, as if not liking what she noted. "There's definitely a possibility."

"Right. I find if there's one, it's not unusual that there's more than one. Likely in your camp too. Having a tracker? We might as well send them our plans in triplicate. You, me, and the kid will be in greater danger. To make this work, we do it my way. I told you, I give an order, you follow it."

He opened his mouth, and she hissed. *This will get annoying real quick if I have to explain everything in detail.*

"I don't much care if you like what I say. I get in, grab the kid, and we both get out alive. That's my mission. I'm good at my job, okay? If I have to get rid of you to save her, I'll do that too. The tracker had to go. We need to be hard to find. Okay?" She punched the words home, hoping he'd grasp the intent. She didn't have time to waste babying him.

From that point on, they drove in relative silence, and she liked it that way. Now she concentrated on the environment around her. The terrain was rugged, the red of the sandy dunes giving way to the olive of scrubby bushes. It was very like the outback.

"Stop us about five miles out. Later on, you can call someone out to collect the vehicle."

Gallagher shot a surprised look at her. "What? How are we supposed to get the child out of here if we don't have the vehicle?"

It took a moment for Tia to realize he hadn't caught on to her thoughts. *He's not been where you have, Tia. Doesn't have your experience in planning operations or surviving them.* "We aren't driving out. That would make us a sitting duck. We're going to have to leg it, Gallagher. Taking advantage of the natural undulations, finding shade during the day and moving at night if we can."

"You're mad!"

Used to outbursts from civilians, Tia waited him out while he questioned her planning.

When he drew breath, she held up a hand. "I know exactly what you're thinking. We're going to be travelling with a child. I know all that. Trust me, I'd make the crossing in ten days by myself, but we need to do it in no more than fifteen. That means walking at night when we'll be harder to spot. Taking shade during the day and hiding. We have to cross into Zambia without being seen, and that's no easy feat. Even when we arrive, we need to get well past the border and reach Livingstone undetected."

"But that's—"

"Around twenty kilometres a day. Yes, which is why there are two of us to help. We may need to carry the girl for distances. I've got nutrition bars in my bag, so the pack will lighten as we travel longer. We need to get to the water hole, and we don't want to be doing that at peak times when the militia might be flying over. On the road, we'll be quick, it's true, but also easier to find and track. All they have to do is jam the roads and they've got us."

He shook his head.

"Look, I did a little bit of digging while in transit. If we fail, the democracy of Zabuti is at stake. Hundreds of thousands of lives, Gallagher. They won't ever get another chance at any quality of life." When the words didn't make him appear to agree, she moved in for the kill. "You know what they do to those who cross them? I'll tell you what we can look forward to. The child will die, and we'll disappear. But not before we suffer. Rape, torture, and slow death for me. You? They'll probably shoot you, then drag your body through the street, televise it, and any hope of a democratic alliance will go poof."

Gallagher steered the car to the side of the road. "Why didn't you warn me?"

"To be honest? You're a G-Man, and I thought you'd know the reasons we couldn't travel by road. What's your specialization?"

He stared at her, shook his head, swiped a hand over his face.

"Cal?"

Now Cal had a decidedly green tinge to his skin. For a moment, Tia was sure he'd vomit, but he controlled it, breathing hard. "I... we need to keep moving." He steered the car back onto the road, and they travelled in silence as questions formed in her mind. The greatest being how much experience he had in the field and whether he'd be an asset or liability.

"Cal? I need to know. What is your specialty?"

"Political sciences."

The answer surprised her, and she blinked. "Okay, so nothing involving guns or planning operations?"

"I can use a gun." He spoke stiffly, and she had to hold in a sigh.

"Okay, tell me what you're rated for."

He smiled. "I carry a Glock."

Again, Tia blinked. "What kind?"

"There's more than one?" His voice rose with surprise, and she wanted to close her eyes in frustration. *A G-Man without even the most basic of skills is to be my partner. Great. Just fucking fabulous!*

Tia had to remind herself he was a pen-pusher in the CIA, but he was all she had. He wasn't an operative who had to deal with life-and-death interactions, even though many people wrongly believed members of the CIA were trained in guns and undercover operations. Most weren't, and clearly Callum Gallagher wasn't a member of the Security Protective Service—those who were.

She ran her hands through her hair. "Okay, do you have it on you?"

He pointed to the console. "It's in there."

With care, Tia opened the hatch and dragged out a hip holster and a small packet of shells in a cardboard box. She wanted to remonstrate, but clearly he didn't have much of an idea about the safest way to store his weapons. She scrutinized the pistol and was pleased it was a small Glock 19. "Huh," she muttered and checked the chamber. At least it was empty. His passport was also stashed in the opening, and she slid it out and into her pocket. They'd need that later on to get out of Zambia if they were forced to run.

At that point, the vehicle veered off the road once more and started on a bumpy track. "Where are we going?" she asked.

"We should be able to park around here. I'll get Trent, my offsider, to come collect it tomorrow."

She waited until they came to a stop, then turned to look at him. "I'm a sniper, Gallagher. Part of my job is to kill people if necessary. You know the child is my mission. If you're going to experience issues with this, I recommend you turn around and leave me to it. I can get her out on my own, though it would be less difficult with a partner. But I need to know now. Are you up to whatever I have to do?"

He stared at her. "They said you were special ops."

"Black ops," she corrected absently. The time came for some tough questions. "I'm part of a team under normal circumstances, but this situation is one where I don't have a backup, not even radio support. I've experience in these situations, Cal, but this isn't my strongest skill. I'll do my best to get all of us to safety in Living-stone, but you're going to have to play your part too. Can you do that?"

Gallagher nodded. "Yeah, I can do that."

A thread of disquiet wound around her, but this was as good as it was going to get. "Good. Then help me out. We need to get my pack, the items you purchased, and my weapons case."

In silence, they completed the unpacking. She pulled the chute bag free and handed it to him, the silk forgotten in the back of the vehicle. "This is the best I can do. Take some of the water. I'll give you some of the protein bars. Put on your pistol and pass me the box of shells." She'd keep them safe. If he needed them, she'd be able to give them back.

"Send a text, then turn off the phone and leave it in the glovebox."

"What?"

"Leave. It. Behind."

"But—"

"Do as I say, Cal. It's necessary, okay?"

When he came closer, she realized she'd forgotten an important step and sighed. "Take off your shirt."

"What?"

"Your shirt. Take it off, then wash with the soap you bought."

When he rolled his eyes, she shook her head. "Your cologne or aftershave or whatever. The scent is strong. We need to wash it off."

"What?"

"The smell will give us away."

Now he winced, understanding her actions. "Sorry."

She supervised his washing, not missing the chiselled physique of the firm trim waist.

Not looking for a man, Tia. Just do the job, get home to safety and your family in Alathea Rangers. Your BOB will still be there at home. And if she needed something breathing, there were always the boys in bars eager for some horizontal time with a willing female partner.

She unsealed her weapons pack and dragged out the knives, sliding one into each boot. "Can you throw?"

When he stared, she knew that was her answer and popped the rest back into their specially made travel case at the bottom of the bag. Next, she extracted her twin pistols. One went into a holster at her hip while the other was suspended from a shoulder pouch.

Last, she dragged out her rifle, scrutinized it and then used the webbing strap so it hung down over her shoulder.

Grabbing her pack, she shrugged it on. The familiar weight settled, and she rubbed the straps. They were old friends.

"Let's head out." She dragged the map from her pants pocket and unfolded it. Taking out her compass, she sighted the direction they'd be moving in, Cal having informed her that Sarah was being held in a camp nearby. There wasn't a lot of cover, but she'd make it work.

They trudged along, him striding along beside her, and she was pleased he wore sensible boots and long pants. The lack of a hat was an issue, but she could help him out with that soon enough. At least he wasn't wearing mirrored shades over his eyes.

FIVE

Cal wasn't quite sure what to make of the woman beside him. She carried the heavy pack he'd struggled to lift with ease. She'd spoken bluntly, her face calm as if she were watching a movie. The whole time, all he could think was *What brought her to this point in her life?*

He thought of his sisters, Jo and Lisa. They were both at home, raising families, and worked part-time. Lisa was a lawyer, and Jo was a nurse. Both were soft, nurturing, yet when he looked at this woman, he read resolve and steely determination in every move she made.

They walked for ages, and then suddenly she stopped him. "Lie down here and be quiet." She shrugged off her pack, stashing it under a scrubby tree at the top of an undulation, then sliding in beside it. "Quick," she hissed, indicating he should follow suit.

The bump in the landscape wasn't quite tall enough to be a hill, but it rose like an ocean wave.

Small rocks scattered the area, and he swept them aside, aware she'd barely moved a muscle since pulling a scope from her pack. Suddenly Cat, as she called herself—and he guessed that wasn't her real name—moved and grabbed her rifle, attaching bits and pieces.

"There's movement," she whispered, and he looked around, wondering how the hell she knew where to look when she pointed.

She lifted her binoculars, and he waited, wondering if he'd get an opportunity to look.

When Cat passed the glasses to him, he peered into the distance. "That's Kezia Matcha. She's a Zabutian of Portuguese extraction, from what I understand. There's been chatter about her being aligned to the militia and particularly the leader." He watched a little longer as the older woman with streaked hair ducked into one of the three small shacks fringing the cleared zone.

"I'd bet Sarah is in one of those sheds," muttered Cat, and he handed her back the glasses.

"So, what do we do next?" In his mind, he foresaw her running in, guns blazing, and his gut clenched hard.

"We wait. Watch what they do and how. The timing is important. We'll only get one shot," Cat answered, and his muscles relaxed a little.

"How do we make camp?"

She turned and speared him with her gaze. "We don't. We wait and watch. If you're tired, you can roll out one of the blankets I've got in the bottom of my bag, but other than that, patience is key."

Not for the first time, he felt a sense of disquiet. This woman was obviously well trained and controlled, but whatever the choice of action came next, there was a likelihood of her using terminal force.

"You'll kill them all?"

She rubbed a hand over her brow. "No. Not necessarily. I don't *kill* everyone. I'd rather not terminate a single damn person. If I can scare them off, then that's better, but at the end of the day, my job is to get the kid out of there. So be quiet and let me do my job." Cat turned back to the view, and her muscles relaxed as if she were ready to rest.

Except he'd bet his last dollar she wouldn't allow herself to lose concentration for even a moment.

IT WAS BAD ENOUGH TO BE LYING HERE WITH SOMEONE WHO thought she was nothing more than a killer for hire. The thought stung—a lot.

And he asks lots of questions, her mind helpfully added.

Not an ideal scenario.

Plus, she was super aware of him there beside her. It took every ounce of concentration to sink into the task, watch the movements as they walked back and forth. Four combatants. Two resting with their ancient .22-calibre rifles on their laps. Lazy and poorly trained. That didn't make them any less dangerous, though.

The woman didn't appear to be carrying anything, but that meant nothing. She might have a pistol under her shirt. Tia kept looking, hoping she'd find an answer. The last man was stocky, with an air of menace about him. His eyes were always moving as if seeking her out. He carried a rifle as well. One she knew well. The R1 FN-FAL battle rifle was an efficient and reliable weapon and had likely been sourced from the South African army. She only hoped it wasn't well cared for, though that would be a slim chance, given he appeared to know what he was doing.

While Tia watched, the man strode forward and spoke with Kezia, who shook her head quickly and retreated to the fire, lifting something and scooping it into a bowl. At the door of the smallest hut, she picked up a bucket as well and disappeared inside.

"Hey, Cal, who's the guy?" She passed the glasses to him and waited long, tense moments, making sure he stayed far enough below the shade to keep him out of sight.

"That's Harold Mubektu, the regional leader of the militia. Worked his way through the ranks but had some experience in the South African army, I believe."

"Damn." There went her hopes that he wouldn't be adequately trained, vain as they'd been.

He handed her back the glasses. "Why?"

"Because unless he leaves, he's going to be my pick for termination first." She turned back, hearing the buzz of an engine in the distance. "Heads-up. Something or someone is on the way," she said and settled back into her hollow.

"We need to get the girl now." He half rose, and she shoved him back down, swallowing a curse.

"No. I don't act in haste. We wait and watch." Her gaze drifted over the view as an old jeep came rumbling into her line of sight. Two men got out; the conversation appeared light-hearted. Kezia, who'd now stepped back into the middle of the congregation, shook her head, answered questions, then retreated to a chair in the shade of another hut. A man came striding out of the second hut, and Tia thanked her training. If she'd rushed in, she'd have likely died, shot by the man who exuded an aura of evil.

"Who's this?" She shoved the eyeglasses back at Cal, who grunted.

"Simon Vorhoek. Second in command of the militia." His tone dripped with distaste, and that reinforced Tia's decision to wait and see. Even as she watched, he climbed into the jeep with the two men, and they drove away.

If only I knew how many others might be hiding in the hut. Tia could wish for the moon, but right then, all she could do was watch and wait for an opportunity.

The chill of the night air settled over her as she watched, the horizon now streaked with orange and violet. "Night's coming in," she muttered, then reached into her pack for a nutrition bar and passed him one as well. "We should eat now."

"Oh, thanks." He didn't sound particularly impressed with the fare, but she shrugged. It would keep them alive and meet the caloric needs on a forced march. *Been there, done that,* she thought. *Got the t-shirt.*

She forced herself to keep up her watch, time ticking by. At some point, she became aware Cal had fallen asleep after relieving himself beyond the bushes. Now that he wasn't annoying her, with the silence only interrupted by the odd *whuff* of his snores, she could plan without having to take time to answer another query. The woman, she'd likely be able to overpower. There was a mile between them and her. She could cover that in a few minutes, but she'd be exposed as she advanced.

Not good. They needed some kind of diversion, but what? The area was flat and open.

The need to get to the hut was urgent. Under cover of darkness, she could head in that direction, sneak over, crawl under the wall. Her small cutters should do the job, as the huts didn't appear to be sturdy. Perhaps she could get the child out without actually being seen.

Long moments passed before she tapped Cal on the shoulder, waking him while at the same time urging him to silence. "Stay here. I need to pee."

The tiny shovel she'd instructed him to use earlier sat by her pack, and she grabbed it up, then slid around the bush before returning, taking a quick sip of water as she considered what she'd tell him.

"I have to get to the hut. Not just yet. And definitely not during daylight. So that leaves later tonight. I've got a small headset I'll wear. You'll have its mate because I'm going to need you to be my spotter. Your job is to watch and let me know if you see anything."

The whole plan was risky. He might miss something, and she'd be caught. Tortured and executed. The kid dead before anyone else could save them. But right then, there weren't many options, which minimized the risks substantially if she could pull it off.

She had only an hour to two in which to teach him what to watch for. What she needed him to warn her about.

SIX

Cal's head buzzed. He needed to listen and strained his ears as he watched her retrieve items from her pack. She stuffed a bar in one pocket, a set of what looked like pliers only with a razor-sharp edge into another. Cat inspected her pistols, checking the actions before loading the magazines, then instructed him to do the same.

Next, she painted her face with a reddish khaki "cake," as she called it. Cat had already explained that by decreasing anything that seemed "out of the ordinary," the chances of them spotting her grew slimmer.

"The headset is short range. I'll be able to hear you, but likely so can they." She jerked her thumb to the huts. "But tonight is our best option. At least the jeep hasn't returned. When I get back here with the kid, be ready to move immediately."

Deep in his bones, Cal felt the danger. It was a palpable tang on his tongue and the rapid beat of his heart, yet when he looked at Cat, he saw none of that. Only determination and calm acceptance.

"If it goes south, get out of here as quickly as you can. Contact your superiors, and they'll know how to contact my office."

She slid away, leaving little to no tracks.

~

Tia held great concern about this move, but there were no other options.

Every step was taken in near silence, eyes scanning and ears straining for signs someone had seen her. Just in the last hour, the woman—Kezia—had retreated into the other building, leaving the two lax guards on duty. The man Cal had called Vorhoek had gone inside as well.

Closer she inched until finally she was beside the shack where the two entered. Carefully she pressed as close to the wall as she dared.

Movement and sounds echoed. Grunts and squeaks. Tia smiled. Sex. Good. They'd likely be occupied for a little while.

She moved to the shack with care. They'd agreed it was likely the place where the child was hidden. Again she listened. Though muffled, sounds of sobs echoed, and Tia removed the sharp plier-like implement from her pocket. She made a small hole and peered within—a single, small figure hunched in the middle.

With great care, Tia cut an access port, keeping her moves silent.

Even as she peeled the thatch away, eyes flashed to her. Tia slipped a finger to her lips. *Shhh.*

She slithered in and took a moment to orient herself, listening for any sounds of movement, then rushed to the child, brandished her knife to release the bonds. "Shhh. I'm here to get you out, but you have to be silent, Sarah," she whispered against the girl's ear.

The little girl stiffened for a moment when Tia took her hand.

"We have to go." She pulled the girl behind her, then replaced the wall she'd cut away. It wouldn't slow them down for long, but anything was better than no chance at this point.

They stayed low with Tia whispering instructions to Sarah along the way, towing her back to Cal. The little girl stumbled twice before Tia lifted the child and carried her while moving quickly and in near silence.

So little time.

The voice in the back of her head urged her on, and once they reached Cal, Tia tugged on her pack and scooped up her rifle. "We have to move quickly. There's a small dip in several kilometres that way." She pointed in the general direction they needed to go. "The ground is hard, so we won't leave tracks, but we're going to have to travel away from our desired resting place before heading in that direction to throw them off the track," Tia explained as they began to move in the dark.

The girl stumbled again, and Tia grimaced. There was no way they'd make two kilometres if the little girl was so uncoordinated. "Cal, tie your pack to mine. Then you carry Sarah." That way her hands were free for the rifle.

He followed her instructions while precious seconds ticked past. Finally satisfied, they moved, this time at a rapid clip, jogging over the ground. She set a hard pace, more than aware that it was punishing for Cal, but there was no other way to make it safely to the location she needed them at tonight.

Changing directions, the pace became easier, the hard surface replacing the sandy ground. "Keep going," she murmured every few minutes while aware that scanning and watching were vital. Just as they reached their desired location, lights shone, and she pushed them down to the ground. "In that hole there. Go."

They did, scrambling. She followed, and only with seconds to spare. The lights flashed, and she controlled her breathing, fingers across her lips, reinforcing to Cal and Sarah the need to remain silent. Her heart thudded against her ribs as she waited, adrenalin coursing through her and her gaze on the light, ready for any action, pistol in hand.

CAL FELT SICK. *CLOSE!* SO DAMNED CLOSE, YET THE WOMAN seemed calm and in control. Was she a robot? Didn't this faze her at all?

He sweated like a pig, felt clammy and sticky, but she'd barely broken a sweat.

Sarah clung to him, her eyes large and her lip trembling. "Shh," he whispered but stopped when Cat glared at him and raised her finger again.

Time passed, and he noted the tension draining from the woman —anxiety he hadn't noticed before. "Okay, we're safe for now," she said. "We're going to hunker down here for an hour or so, and then we'll move again. They'll stop searching soon, I think. We hid our tracks, so this is more a case of them fanning out, I'd guess. It wasn't the main guy looking, and the others don't appear well drilled and don't think broadly."

Now she turned to the girl in his arms. "Hi, Sarah. Sorry we couldn't talk before. I'm called Cat. I'm here to help you, and so is Cal, who's snuggling you."

"How do you know my name?"

Cat grinned. "Your daddy sent us here. He's really worried about you, and because there's a lot of danger, he needed someone special to get you out. That's my job. Cal is here to help me."

"When can we go home?" Sarah whined.

"Hmm, that's hard to explain. I'll try later, but right now, I have to keep an eye on what's happening, okay? But you're safe here with us."

"Then why don't we stay here tonight?" Cal thought they could probably all do with the rest, and he was reasonably sure Cat hadn't slept earlier in the night either. She'd been peering through the binoculars when he went to sleep and had woken him gently.

"No. We have to get moving. There's a location nearby. It's about ten kilometres from their base. There's no water, which is why I made you get some for us, Cal, but it's rocky. We can hide out for the day. Get some rest and be reasonably safe. We'll take turns at keeping watch."

He frowned. "Ten kilometres? That's like—" He calculated it in his head. "—six and a half miles?"

She shrugged. "Not quite. Yes, it's a lot, but doable. Especially if we intend to survive. Sarah? Are you okay?"

The little girl trembled. "I want my daddy."

Cat's eyes narrowed, and she crouched down to address the child at eye level. "I know, sweetie. But I need to make sure you're okay. Not hurt or anything." She looked the little girl over, and he was pretty sure she'd take whatever care she had to if the little girl had been injured. But she appeared satisfied as she scanned the little girl.

Sarah shook her head. "They tied me to a stick. I had to go to the toilet in a bucket." There was a wealth of disgust in the child's voice.

Cat smiled. "Okay, that sounds like it sucked. Bet you were brave, though, right? Were they nasty to you?"

The girl screwed her eyes up tight. "Only the man. The one with the big gun. He was mean and said horrible stuff like Daddy would have to do what he wanted or...." Here she made a slicing movement with her hand and the sound of a knife sliding over the flesh.

Foolish behaviour. The little girl had a spine. She'd not screamed or carried on when he'd picked her up. She'd simply hung on, and he thought she'd done the same when Cat had entered the hut. He'd watched from his vantage point, and none of the guards had clearly seen or heard anything.

"Bet you're hungry, right?" He reached into his pocket and pulled out a crushed candy bar, holding it out to her. Not for the first time, Cal breathed a sigh of relief that they'd gotten her out of the mess, but could they keep her safe now? The fact that he didn't know was unnerving.

"You two take a break. Sleep if you can manage it. I'll stand watch." Cat moved away as if checking the safety of their location before climbing up a rock and peering over the edge.

He slumped down, and the little girl snuggled in close. Within moments they were both asleep.

SEVEN

Tia yawned. The ten-kilometre march had been uneventful but incredibly slow, and now they were at the rock site she'd found on the map. It was 0400 hours, she noted, checking her watch.

"Step back and let me see what's inside." She scoured the tiny niche in the rocks, tossing in pebbles. "That should scare anything up that's inside and large."

As Tia made to enter, Cal grabbed her hand. "Snakes," he muttered.

"Yup. I'm watching out. Looking for anything like the Bibron's stiletto, black mamba—"

Cal's eyes widened. "What are you, a walking encyclopedia?"

She laughed and watched as he blinked. "Not exactly, but I have a near eidetic memory. I checked the poisonous creatures of this area, snakes and scorpions and so on. The most poisonous spiders of the continent aren't found in this region normally." Then Tia grabbed the compact torch from her pack.

"Why didn't you use that before?" He nudged the hand holding the illuminated object.

"Because if I had, we might as well phone them and give them our GPS coordinates and hand ourselves over. Now, I need to go in so we can set ourselves up."

Leaving the man and child outside, she moved with caution within the tiny area. It would be a squeeze, but as they'd mostly be sleeping, they would manage. She scoured every inch and, finally satisfied they'd be safe, ducked her head out and waved them in. Before hunkering down, she rolled one of the rocks toward the entrance with a grunt so it obscured them from view. "This will give us some cover if necessary. It'll also shade the cavern. Grab a blanket each and roll them down while I set up."

Tia arranged a screen of scrubby brush over the entrance, then set up her rifle on the folding legs.

"That's a big gun," said Sarah as she yawned.

Tia drew back and frowned. "It is. It's also dangerous, Sarah. You don't touch it or my pistols or Cal's either. Okay? We're here to get you safely back home, but there's a couple rules you need to know and follow. Stay near me. Don't wander off unless I tell you specifically. Can you do that?"

The little girl nodded wearily. "I'll stay near you."

"If you're hurt, bitten, or anything else, tell me straight away. I can't look after you unless you talk to me. If I'm not there, you tell Cal." Tia bit her lip, trying to think over what else she needed to tell the girl immediately. Her thoughts turned to the passports shoved in her shirt. "If we run into someone, don't speak unless I say it's okay. Your name, if anyone asks and you have to answer, is Sarah Warner. I'm your mother, Catherine Warner, but people call me Cat, and Cal's my boyfriend."

He started, his face shocked, and she nearly laughed at his round eyes and surprised expression.

She let the mirth die away and turned back to the child, thinking over her list of instructions. "Last and most important. When I tell you to do something, you have to do it right away without asking questions, okay? We've got a long way to travel and have to do it at night for the next few days. It's not going to be easy, but it'll keep you safe. You just have to follow my rules so those nasty people don't get you again."

The girl shuddered, and Tia wondered if she was laying it on too thick. *Perhaps, but she has to be aware and alert.*

"Cal, you're the on first watch. Wake me in three hours. Then you can have a spell too. Sarah? I want you to sleep at the back of the cave. Settle on in." She waited for the girl to lie down, thankful they'd taken a moment for a comfort stop outside. Getting out now would present more of a challenge, and she'd rather they went at least in twos. There were plenty of large animals around the area; they'd seen scats and heard sounds enough to disquiet Tia.

When the little girl settled, Tia lay down lengthways so her head was butted up against the large rock she'd rolled into position.

"What do I do?" Cal looked at her, his gaze earnest.

She glanced at her watch again. "Wake me at 0700... um, seven in the morning. Listen for vehicles, voices, and critters. Big and small. Wake me if you're concerned."

Resting her head on her pack, she closed her eyes, settled her breathing, and fell into a light doze.

THE DAY PASSED SLOWLY, TAKING TURNS NAPPING, KEEPING Sarah occupied when she woke. Toileting was difficult, and they all held on by sleeping most of the day away. At three in the afternoon, Cal opened his eyes once more to note the way Cat was watching him.

"Shh... Sarah's asleep. Scoot over so we can talk."

He moved close to her, and she peered outside again. "There's movement out there. I can hear vehicles. They've been doing circuits for the last ten minutes or so." Cat spoke quietly, her face calm, but she peered intently through the glasses. "Three vehicles. One possibly a jeep. If they get much closer, I'm going to have you wake Sarah and keep her quiet and hidden. We don't want to be cornered."

He nodded, well aware she was preparing him in case things went bad quickly.

He hunched beside her, taut and ready to act at her command, when he heard the sound of engines. Cal opened his mouth, but she waved a hand, stopping him.

Turning back so their gazes collided, she shook her head. "Wait," she mouthed.

One finger, then a second shot up.

Two what? Cars? Long moments passed, then the sound of raised voices.

"Sarah. Get Sarah." Urgency threaded her whisper, and he moved just as the sound of a gunshot echoed.

The girl's eyes opened, and she shot upwards and opened her mouth. He slid a hand over it. "Quietly, Sarah. Be quiet," he whispered into her ear, and she nodded her understanding.

Now another engine roared to life and sped off.

He glanced at Cat as she slumped over, then held up three fingers. He exhaled.

"Too close," Cat muttered. "We'll give it ten, and then I'll check."

He read the concern in her eyes, and understanding flared. They'd shot someone, and she didn't want him or Sarah to see. That stung on one level. Under normal circumstances, the woman would be clinging to him for reassurance and safety, but their roles were reversed this time. He felt... strangely adrift and aggrieved. *That doesn't make sense, Cal.* He released the thought to the universe and concentrated on the here and now.

Time passed slowly, and the little girl clung to him, her body quivering.

Cat passed out three of the protein bars. It was like eating cardboard.

"These taste horrible," whined Sarah.

Cat smiled. "I know. Imagine eating them for Christmas dinner. I did that once, in Cambodia. Sticky and smelly weather that day. I hadn't showered in over three days, and it kept raining. That was a Christmas."

Sarah's eyes rounded. "You were in Cambodia? Daddy went there once. Brought me back a doll. He stayed in a hotel. Why didn't you?"

Cat laughed, the sound a tinkle. "I was in the rainforest on a... trek."

Cal didn't miss how she paused for a moment, then answered. It probably wasn't a lie. It just wasn't the whole story, he was sure. In the two days they'd spent together, he'd already seen how she carefully answered questions—especially those about her and her experiences.

They ate in silence and drank some of the water they'd toted in.

"Sarah, I've got some clothes I want you to change into," Cat said. "It's going to be hot and uncomfortable, but it's part of the plan to keep you safe."

This time, Cat rooted around in the pack she'd thrust on him, made from the pouch she'd kept her parachute in. She handed Sarah the light tracksuit, socks, and sneakers. "Get into this. If they don't fit, I have a plan."

Cal turned his back, giving the girl privacy, and waited until Cat tapped him on the shoulder. "I need to go out there. You stay here and look after Sarah."

With economical motions, she stripped away the scrubby bushes she's set up in front of the rifle, folded it down, and laid it on top of her pack. With a glance back, then a nod, she pushed through the doorway.

Moments passed long. *At least it's not summer.* If it was, the temperatures right then out there would be unbearable. As it was, things were warm without the cover of the bushes to shade the entire cavern.

When Cat returned, her mouth was grim, her hands grimed with dirt and something wet. Her lips were tight and her eyes narrowed.

"Bastards." Then she glanced at the child. "Don't repeat that," she growled.

The little girl nodded, seeming for the first time to be wary of the woman in the doorway.

"Sarah, do you need to go to the bathroom?"

The little girl nodded that she did, and Cat sighed. "Cal, I need you to come with me first."

She dragged him out, then moved in front of him. "They shot one of the guards. He's down there. I can't bury him because the vultures, or lack of, will give away that we found him. So we go around the top, so the kid doesn't see. Sarah needs the bathroom, so I'll take her downwind. We've got another couple hours before dark, but I want to be out by no later than 1730 hours—uh, five thirty in civvie talk. That gives us enough time to traverse this section and get the lay of the land. Then we head on."

He nodded, aware of the dangers they faced from large predators. "Where are we headed?"

"I'll show you on the map once we're back inside."

Together they returned to the cave, and she ushered Sarah out, dragging the child well away from the body, he deduced. When they returned, they settled inside on the blankets, Cat pulling the bushes back. "To keep the temps down." She smiled at Sarah.

They pored over the map, and Cat drew a line with her finger. "This is where we need to go." She pointed to a spot well short of a riverbed.

"If we go all the way, we can access water."

Cat shook her head. "No. We need to stay away from that for now. They'll be looking for us to be close to a water source, so they'll be hunting in those zones specifically. I researched some significant spots nearby and think this will serve." She pointed to a spot on the map. "Here."

"But—"

"We'll be about four kilometres—two and a half miles—to water.

Not too far, but they won't expect us to remain that close if we're not on the banks."

Cal scratched his head. "You seem pretty sure."

She shook her head. "I can't be. But watching the guards' actions, the lax way they acted makes me think tactical planning isn't their strong point. I think they thought Sarah was a soft target and no one would be game enough to hunt for the location where they stashed her." She rubbed her chin and glanced at the child before focusing back on him. "Hell, Vorhoek was having sex with the woman in the shack next to where they had Sarah." He heard the distaste in her voice at their actions and wondered if others could too or if his ability to read her was due to the ongoing close proximity. "They don't really know where we are, I'm assuming, based on what we saw earlier. They're guessing. They've got no intel or idea of our location. We've been off the grid since I made you leave your phone behind in the car."

He blinked. "That didn't even occur to me."

"No. That's just another reason I'm so good at my job. I *do* think about all these things. It's my job to read the situation, draw conclusions, and plan based on those facts. So, drink your water, and make sure you're ready when I say. We've got about an hour until we move out."

He watched as she repacked everything into the kit bag and once again wondered at her history. "What did you do before?"

She turned back. "What do you mean?" Her gaze turned canny. "I could tell you, but it would scare your socks off."

Cal frowned. "No, I really do want to know. You weren't a SEAL because you told me you were in some crack unit in the army."

The laughter faded from her face. "SASR. Special Air Services Regiment."

Answering with a grunt, Cal leaned in. "You said that before. What exactly does it mean?"

Settling down on her backside opposite him, she beckoned Sarah close, as she'd just woken. "It's a branch of the Australian army, with specialist training in remote and challenging locations. We enter war zones and make things happen, Cal. It's not pretty, but it's not just a job. It's... it's a calling, I guess. We take the chances to keep people alive."

Pondering her words, he closed his eyes and considered how they'd met. "You parachuted in."

Surprise bloomed on her face. "I did." She nodded. "A HALO jump."

He waited for her to elaborate, and when she didn't, he raised his brows in a manner that broadcast he was waiting.

"High Altitude Low Opening. I jumped at 15,000 feet. Or thereabouts."

He gaped, and the little girl grabbed Cat's face. "Why did you do that? Were you scared?"

Again, Cat laughed, this time at Sarah's question. "I did it because I was coming to get you out of that shack. Yes, I'm always a little bit scared, but I've done heaps. In lots of places. America, England, Iraq, and Afghanistan. Cook Islands."

The girl practically bounced. "You've been to lots of countries."

"I have," she answered, but this time her lips drooped.

Something happened in one of those far-flung countries which propelled her away from the life she'd built. He wondered if she'd tell him about it sometime.

He nearly laughed because how long did he expect they'd be together? And when would they have the opportunity to talk in safety?

EIGHT

They reached the dip in the hill, and once again, Tia checked to ensure their safety from snakes and creatures. "I'd rather a cave again, but there aren't any around here, not that I can see easily on my map. So we're going with good, old-fashioned ingenuity. Sarah, grab the blankets and put them on the base under that tree over there."

Now she turned to Cal. "I need some camouflage. Sticks, twigs, and branches. Don't drag through. Lift them in case they have a drone. We're going to build a hide."

He hurried off, following her instructions.

Meanwhile, she toted her bag and popped it under the brush, not on a blanket but beside it.

"Why do you carry that? It's heavy. We could kill an animal for food."

Sarah's innocent question actually hurt Tia. The girl had no idea that the bag contained a range of things that would keep them alive, including a couple stun grenades, munitions for the rifle, and pistols. It carried essential first aid supplies and even individual water purification systems in the form of life-sustaining purification straws.

"It's got stuff I need inside it, Sarah. Things that will keep us healthy while we get you to safety."

Sarah nodded." Okay. Do I get one like Cal's?"

Tia narrowed her eyes. "Do you reckon you could manage one?"

The girl considered, then nodded. "I could carry some water and food for you."

A smile split Tia's face. "Okay. While we rest today, I'll see what I can come up with." The girl had proven far more resilient today, acting as if the situation was an adventure, and right then, Tia was grateful for the mindset. It was much easier to work with someone who wanted to assist than one who simply expected everyone to save them. It seemed it didn't matter the age when they were determined.

Once the hide was erected, she ushered them in. Even as they settled on the blankets, they heard a sound, and Tia's gut froze. The roar echoed in the hour between first light and the true dawn.

A golden creature loped down close enough that they would be in danger with a careless action. "Quiet, everyone," Tia breathed as the animal stopped and scented the air. Her fingers moved instinctively toward her pistol.

It turned massive golden eyes and a maw that might swallow Sarah whole in their direction as if sensing their location.

The long tail flicked once, twice, then a third time before the creature turned and headed for the water.

"Too close," she breathed, and Sarah grabbed her hand.

"A lion. A real, up close lion. Wait till I tell my friends at home." The excited words ended on a squeak, and Tia had to shush her.

"We're not totally safe here, Sarah," Cal offered. "Lots of animals come down, including elephants, so you'll need to stay quiet."

Tia glanced over Sarah's head and mouthed, "Thank you," to Cal. He'd said what she'd been grappling for. It was bad enough that Tia had chosen an exposed area to shelter in during the day, but their options had been limited. She'd rather find hillocks and caverns, but with none around, she'd had to make do with the sparse trees to shelter beneath.

Without a word, they settled Sarah down, waiting for the sounds of sleep. Before Tia could suggest she'd take first watch, he turned. "How did you end up in the Alathea Rangers, Cat?"

She sighed. The weight of knowledge was heavy enough that it almost pulled her under a few times, but Cal seemed to want to know, and the need to share some of the load rose. "A couple of us were in the Cook Islands. We'd heard about traffickers using one island in particular as a base. We jumped in." She gazed out over the landscape, wondered how best to explain what happened. Oh, she could do it in military speak, but he was a civilian, and it would be like rubbing his face in the knowledge. She had no intentions of doing that. "There were five of us. Handpicked. Me as point, sniper... however you want to describe it. Len, my... partner. Three other guys. New and raw. We were supposed to show them how missions work outside the bubble of training." Tears stung her eyes. "Len and I were... you know. It wasn't really allowed, but we worked together, trained together. Things happened, and before we both knew it, we were in a relationship. The mission started badly. One of the guys broke his hand before the jump, so we had to send him home. Went on, just the four of us. I'd already outlined the jump, planned it meticulously. It went badly. Len... he didn't come home. Or I guess he did, but in a body bag."

She turned away because she knew tears were almost there, ready to appear if she let down her guard.

"There was an inquiry. The head honchos found out about Len and me. They questioned my leadership. Said I'd been lax. What really happened was the two guys collaborated on their story after the jump went wrong. Said I'd given conflicting orders. I was going to be court-martialled until the pilot and crew of our transport stepped up. Their orders were to fly on, refuel, and offer support to the local forces. They got wind of what was going on and gave statements. But by then...." Tia shrugged.

Cal put a hand on her shoulder, and she bowed her head. "Cat?"

"It's all old news." If only that were the truth, but her entire life was a series of missteps, accidents, and horror.

"Come on, Cat, you can tell me."

God knew she wanted to. "I got out. I'd heard about my boss, Cara, putting the force together, and she made contact. We'd sort of crossed paths a year or so before when I was seconded to the SEALs for six months."

"She offered you a job?"

"Yeah. I needed space and a new beginning. One where I wasn't a grunt with no brains who'd fucked up. As far as anyone much knows, I just disappeared off the face of the earth."

"Has that given you peace?"

Tia turned to look at him. "Don't tell me you're also a shrink."

He laughed softly. "No. Although I did attend therapy training for a couple sessions. To learn about the psychology of it."

Amusement filled her. "The CIA sent you to therapy, huh? So, you could"—she made air quotes with her fingers—"learn about it."

Cal shrugged. "They send us off on ranges of courses. Whatever helps us to be efficient in the field."

"You know, we should get some sleep. I can take first watch."

Cal gazed off into the vista beyond. "Okay. Wake me when you're ready for a break."

Tia waited as he settled himself, head on her pack. "Don't mind, do you?" he asked.

She returned the shrug. "Only if you don't mind sleeping on stun grenades and munitions."

He bolted upright. "You don't...?"

With a nod, Tia explained, "I carry all sorts of goodies in my bag. But really, they're safe as they are. So get comfortable, have a rest. You're going to need it. I want to pick up the speed a bit tonight."

He growled and settled himself while she waited.

He slept finally, and she allowed herself to consider the last few years—the things she'd purposely blanked out. Len's death had been painful, but even so, she'd completed her mission. It was only when the two new recruits had falsified their statements, claiming she'd given conflicting orders, that she'd realized she didn't belong. Even in the SASR, she was the square peg in a round hole.

The newbies lied to cover up that they'd refused to follow her lead—not uncommon among many men in the army still. A hangover from times when women were only good on the battlefield as nurses and to make cups of tea, she guessed.

Both of them had been dishonourably discharged once the truth came out. But mud, once slung, stuck like glue. The men who'd known her, served with her, argued against her court-martial. But her eventual actions felt right. She'd walked away from the family she'd built in the SASR because some of the men questioned Tia's authority after those events. In the end, she hadn't so much as taken the easy option of resigning as much as minimizing the damage to the regiment.

What Cara had offered was a different kind of family. Tight when the chips were down, but Tia knew, deep in her soul, that she'd not yet let them fully into the spaces she kept hidden. It hurt too much to trust.

As the hours passed, she noted another lion and what appeared to be elephants on the horizon. Sarah and Cal slept and she kept watch, knowing they needed far more rest than she did. She'd been trained to exist without sleep. Hell, when she'd been doing her SASR selection course, they'd been forced to stay awake for four days without food and carry out activities. This wasn't quite as trying.

By the time midday beat down, she'd allowed her mind to find the calm inner centre once more. She shook Cal. He woke with a grunt, and she sighed. "You're going to have to learn to wake up quieter," she muttered, and he pulled a face.

"Sure. Yeah," Cal swiped a hand over his features and took the water bottle she handed him. "Anything interesting happen?"

"A lion, some elephants. Not much else."

He stared at her, then shook his head.

"Nothing exceptional. It's how we roll, Cal Gallagher. Now, let me sleep until 1600, or four o'clock for you non-military types. Then we'll start preparing for the night."

He gave a nod, moved off the blanket, and she slithered down, resting her head on her pack and rubbing the straps once more as if they were her security blanket. When she closed her eyes, she concentrated on breathing. In. Out. Relaxing muscles.

Finally her mind quieted, and she drifted off.

CAL WATCHED CAT DROP INTO A LIGHT SLUMBER. AN ENIGMA was the best description, he thought. The tale of why she'd left the army was only part of the story, he was sure. There was more.

"Insular," he muttered and considered her face. Her features were delicate, her skin pale beneath the light tan, with high cheekbones and a soft mouth that he felt the sudden urge to touch.

His eyes moved to Sarah. Sweet and trusting. Innocent. He knew Cat pulled her punches around the child, and for the first time, he wondered how on earth they'd ensure she remained innocent through what lay ahead.

If Vorhoek or those in charge of the militia found them, there'd be no innocence left, and while he was pretty sure Cat could handle herself, she was, after all, only one single woman.

One who was strong but very damaged. There was more to Cat, and he wondered how he might get her to open up. Then Cal pulled himself together. "You aren't auditioning for a date, you cretin." He'd have to gain control of whatever was affecting his mind and libido.

Sighing, he leaned back to the shrub they'd built the hide on. He had hours left of his watch, and there was lots to see if Cat's version was correct.

OVER THE NEXT FEW NIGHTS, THE RAGTAG GROUP SETTLED INTO a routine. Walk or jog as far as they could, following Tia's compass, finding suitable hiding spots before dawn broke and then hunkering down during the day. Sarah, it appeared, was a reasonably athletic girl. She could walk for hours, but even she had her limits.

On the sixth day, the girl whined about walking. "I hate this. Can't we stop for one day and just stay still? I'm tired."

Tia couldn't say she blamed her. It was a pretty punishing schedule she'd set, but they needed to reach the border within the next few days. In her bones, she just knew any later than that and the militia would work out the group was on foot. That increased the danger a lot. As it was, she wasn't sure a team wouldn't be waiting for her wherever.

What she did find, though, was an abandoned hut on the morning of the tenth day. Though it went against every facet of her training, Tia called a halt at 0300.

"Stay here," she told Cal, and he dragged out his pistol. Over the last few days, he'd become far more adept and aware of the dangers that surrounded them.

Tia entered the hut and scoped it out. No snakes, no scorpions, so why was it empty? Even as she left the hut, questions flowed. "Hey, Cal? It's empty, but I don't get why."

"Where are we?" he queried. She pointed out their location on the map, and he smiled.

"Oil fields. Over that way." The ridge they should have traversed rose like a mound of black and blue against the inky ebony of the sky, dotted with bright diamonds.

"Huh?"

"I didn't realize we were going to come quite this close," he muttered. "This is the reason the militia didn't want to give up control. The fields are worth billions to them. The royalties they earned kept them in weaponry and, from time to time, even mercenaries."

"Fuck." Then she slid a hand over her mouth as Sarah giggled.

"You swear a lot, Cat. Maybe you need a jar. Daddy has one for the staff in Brisbane." Sarah's grin settled her nerves a little. But it also made her wonder if the use of the hut for the day was the best option. She knew the little girl craved normality, but the danger was always close, and if the militia had controlled the oil fields, there was no knowing if someone was keeping an eye on this hut.

They could report back.

Then the militia could take them by surprise.

Turning to Cal, she opened her mouth.

"The government has been patrolling these regions since they regained control. I can't say for sure that we'd be safe, but a day in a proper structure would be beneficial for all of us." Cal spoke wisely, but how would they manage the watches? "What's wrong?"

"The walls make it almost impossible to see."

Cal scratched his head. "You could make peepholes in the thatch."

She bit her lip, torn. To be honest, she wanted the little girl to have some normality, but she needed the safety of the vantage point. The holes weren't the worst idea ever, but neither were they the best.

In the end, Tia simply shrugged. "I need my pliers." Then she set about making large enough holes that they'd be able to gain enough warning to at least give them a chance.

The little girl squealed her excitement as they made up the beds, though the pleasure dissipated when Tia produced more protein bars. "I want something different." Tia had to restrain the urge to roll her eyes.

"I know, sweetie. But it's all we have until we reach Livingstone."

"Why do we have to go there?" Sarah moaned.

Tia ground her teeth, having already explained to Sarah this was where they'd be able to speak to someone who could help them find a way home. "I've already explained to you. The bad guys are looking for us. We have to get there so we can contact your daddy, but far enough away that the bad guys can't get to us." Tia looked to Cal, who simply shrugged.

Once the sparse meal was done, Tia excused herself. She needed to go to the toilet, find water to replenish their supplies, and wanted to scout as much of the area as she could. This hut felt awfully convenient, and convenience was something she didn't trust.

The remains of another hut lay just beyond, and she made her way over, squatted down, and peered beneath. Flies swarmed whatever was below the destroyed thatch, and she frowned, scenarios forming in her mind. At least one spiked her adrenalin and would urge them back out into the bush and scouting for another location. They'd done well hiding from the militia so far. Twice they'd been within reaching distance, but Tia's camouflage had saved them; however, she couldn't and wouldn't rely on luck. "Eventually it runs out," she muttered to the tiny puff of wind that eddied around her body.

With her torch in hand, she shoved at the thatch. The sight beneath was horrifying.

Tia scooted back, well aware they couldn't stay in this location. The militia had been here. Predators would come looking soon as the stench of a rotting body filled her nostrils.

Hightailing it back to the hut was the only option, and Tia quickly attended to her needs before she hurried inside. Cal looked up, and she noted Sarah was already fast asleep on the makeshift bed. "Wake her up. We have to get out of here."

"But she's just—"

Tia was shaking her head. "There are dead bodies in a collapsed hut about twenty metres behind this shack. Rotting dead human bodies," she clarified. "It looks like a militia hit. If we stay, we're either in for a visitor in the form of a predator at the door, or we'll be found."

He blanched and nodded, standing up and waking Sarah, who complained.

With her blood thrumming through her veins, Tia worked to blank out Sarah's complaints of "I'm tired" and "I don't wanna go anywhere" until Tia snapped.

"Sarah, there's dead people, killed by the men chasing us, just outside, okay? I don't much care that you're tired right now. We have to move, and you have to be quiet."

Turning to Cal, she grabbed his bag. "You carry her. I'll take your bag."

His lips thinned, but nonetheless, he picked up the girl, who'd finally quieted. "Where are we going?"

She hadn't planned to make for the border region tonight, but the fear that had bloomed near the bodies crystallized in her mind. "We've made better time than I'd expected these last few days, so we're going to head for the border. We can't cross tonight because I need time to formulate a plan. That means I need to be able to see the set-up. Find a hole we can exploit. Besides, it's too late in the night, and if we were going to try the border now, there'd be questions." Indeed, even as they moved, she felt the coming of dawn, saw the lightening of the sky. She really didn't want her little group in anyone's sight.

"I want to be sure where we make the crossing is as safe as possible. I can't just trot through with this hardware, so we need another way. The place I have in mind is about six kilometres. Hard walking, but if we can get there, there are places we can shelter by the looks of it."

With Sarah riding piggyback on Cal and Tia leading the way, they moved with speed, the whole time Tia cursing herself. The holes in the side of the hut, if they checked, would be a giveaway to anyone with half a brain that they'd been here.

About ten minutes in, Sarah finally stopped complaining. Tia thanked her lucky stars for that, because now they were moving into an area that was going to be populated.

This could very well be the most dangerous part of their journey. People surrounding them, and they wouldn't know until far too late if any were militia sympathisers.

The whole time they walked, Tia's mind churned.

Her feet hurt by the time they'd reached the destination she had in mind, and her eyes swept the area. They were just out of the township, and she swept the area with her gaze. Boulders rose up toward the sky, and she urged Cal over, played the torch over the rocks, checking for snakes and predators. Finally assured it was safe, she moved in.

Expecting caverns, she searched the ridge, finding an egress set well back and high enough up that they'd have the advantage of sight.

They climbed up in silence, and Tia waved Cal and Sarah to the side, allowing her to advance. Once again, the cave wasn't large, but they would fit with a little extra room than they'd had that first night. It was a couple metres up the rock face, so not immediately able to be seen, and for the first time that night, Tia wanted to relax. Satisfied it was empty, she called out, "You can come in."

Cal carried the child in, and he settled Sarah at the back once again on the bed of blankets. The little girl had fallen asleep, and for that, Tia was grateful. She'd refined down to a wisp, and Tia gnawed her lip. The trip had been challenging. The nutrition bars were sufficient for their needs but not much more.

"You want bushes," Cal murmured, and she shook her head.

"No. Not yet." Tia needed to collect something to obscure the front of the egress, but dawn had already broken. If anyone saw her, she could claim to be a backpacker since her face was unknown, but she hesitated. A thin story, but keeping Sarah and Cal out of sight for as long as possible was now key to their success.

Retreating once inside, she'd just found cover when the sound of an engine split the air. Binoculars in hand, she watched as an old battered vehicle drove slowly past the mound. A look at the driver's face reinforced the wisdom of her decision. *Vorhoek.* He carried three men with him, each armed with the ubiquitous R1s.

"Dammit, I had hoped we'd have escaped him," Cal breathed.

She held up a hand, silencing him as the men clambered from the now stationary vehicle. Tia's hands moved for the pistols, and she cursed that she hadn't taken the time to set up her rifle. "Go back. Stay by Sarah."

He followed her instructions with barely a whisper, and she steeled herself, fearing what might yet happen.

Time passed while she remained still, fingertips hovering over the familiar shape of the grip. The men outside clattered around, their searching uncoordinated, and she watched as Vorhoek gave the command to return to the vehicle. There they conversed for several minutes.

Tia wished she'd had a tac-vest, her trusty helmet, and a sub-machine gun on hand. She could have neutralized the threat long enough for them to make their escape. *Maybe.*

Her mind tore apart the holes in that thinking.

You're exposed. Someone might see or hear. You'd have to take the vehicle, and then when you're stopped at the border crossing, how are you going to explain that you're driving a militia vehicle?

When they finally climbed back into the vehicle, the tension in her body was wound tighter than a violin string. The car roared off, and she released a puff of breath. "Far too close," she muttered and turned.

Cal nodded, his eyes wide. "How are we getting out of here, Cat?"

"I'm working on a plan," she muttered.

Cal's eyes widened farther, and she bit her lip, well aware that all the plans she'd made prior were now for nothing. She needed intel, and she needed it quickly. Except how would she find it? Who the hell could she ask?

NINE

Cat rested against the mouth of their cave, and Cal took a moment to watch her. Wondering at the way she took on total responsibility not just for her actions but also his and Sarah's.

"Cat?"

She turned. "What's wrong?" Her face was tense, and the concern she carried like a cloak around herself washed over Cal like a wave.

"How did you come to join your regiment? The army?"

She blinked. Cal noted how she'd done that before when considering a question she didn't want to answer. Maybe it was his CIA training coming out. His understanding of the psychology of her actions intrigued him.

"What do you want to know?"

He moved closer. "Tell me about growing up in Australia. I've always wanted to visit."

She turned and speared him with a glance. "Hot. Wet. Long."

Her three-word answer was strange, as if acknowledging the time before she'd joined the army was a different life. He frowned. "Tell me about your family."

She stilled, and he wondered if she realized it was a huge tell. "I don't have one. They're all dead. Have been for a long time."

He took the hint, for now. Instead, he settled back. "Huh. I grew up in California. Just north of Los Angeles, in Santa Clarita. Great place, good people. The safest city in California."

Her eyes gleamed. "You got siblings?"

He nodded. "Twin sisters, Jo and Lisa. Lisa's a lawyer specializing in tax while Jo's a nurse—a midwife, just returned after her second baby. Then there's Micah, my baby brother. He's at Caltech, studying biochemistry. He's damn smart."

She nodded. "Your parents?"

He sighed. "Mom passed when I was eighteen—breast cancer. Dad's in law enforcement and getting ready to retire. Not sure what he's going to do after that. He's been rattling around the old home by himself for fifteen years and complaining how now that it's just him, he doesn't need a big old rancher."

"I grew up... or rather started out on a property. Cane. Sugar cane," she explained, her gaze far away. "My dad was a third-generation farmer, and as the oldest, he said it was mine someday to take over. When I was eight, things changed. He changed. Overnight he stopped coming home. Mum had the two of us at home. Me and my sister. She tried to keep things together. Then one day, Dad came home in the middle of the day. He was high. It was school holidays and hot, so Lauren and I were outside in the pool. Dad called us in."

His gut clenched. He didn't know why except the look on Cat's face—impassive, as if she were reading from a script—tore at him. "What happened?"

"He had the gun his dad had used in the war. He'd taken it off the wall and cleaned it, loaded it up. He shot Mum first. Through the gut. I remember watching her fall and Lauren screaming. Dad yelling at her to shut up so he could think and saying how she should have just stopped nagging him.

Cal's fingers curled at the pain the young girl must have experienced.

"She wasn't dead. Not yet." She picked at an invisible bit of lint on her filthy pants. "I crawled over and put my hand on her stomach. The hole... I remember the heat and the smell. The way it pulsed as her life just flowed away. She told me to get Lauren out."

Cal didn't know what to say. Cat couldn't have had a clue how her life was going to change in a split second. He reached out, though, and took her hand, noting the frigid temperature of her skin.

"Dad turned on Lauren next. She was screaming. Terrified. I tried to reach her, was halfway across the room when he got her. He shot her in the face." Now she zoned out on him for several long and fraught seconds, as if reliving those moments. "Her head just kind of melted away. Spattered the walls with bits of skin and bone and brain. Then he went for me, got me in the side, and I fell down behind the chair. He didn't know it wasn't enough to kill me, and I lay there, really still and waiting for him to come get me. I guess he must have realized what he'd done, because then he turned the gun on himself. Blew his brains out like the loser he'd become." Now fires burned in the depths of her eyes. "I was so scared. I stayed really still until I was sure, then crawled over to Mum, but she'd died. I hurt so bad because he'd taken everything. The police showed up, but it was too late, and I was too little to save them. I was in hospital when they buried Mum and Lauren. I don't know when they cremated the bastard. I don't really care what happened to him. He's in a wall somewhere in the cemetery, but I wish he'd rotted." Fury gave her words a sharp edge, and his heart ached for the little girl who'd overcome so much already. Had lost too many people she'd cared for. *It's no wonder she remains remote and in control.*

She spoke again, surprising him. "They should have left him out in the field so at least his body would serve some kind of purpose." Cat closed her eyes and settled her head against the side of the cave. Silent tears he doubted she was even aware of rolled down her cheeks. He wanted to comfort her. "I've not talked about it in years. The psych guys at enlistments poked and prodded, but I didn't break. How come I told you?"

There was a wealth of disgust in her words, and he laughed. "Because you needed to." He reached out, touched one of the silvery droplets, and wiped it away. Her eyes flashed open. It wasn't fear, just a recognition of the invisible thread of emotion that now bound them together.

"I don't have time to fall in like, Cal. I don't have the luxury of that high. And I certainly don't do relationships."

It didn't matter whether she did or didn't because he was clearly two steps ahead of her. His thumb swiped the soft skin of her chin. "I'm intrigued by you, Cat. I want to know more about you."

She shook her head. "It's like a form of Stockholm syndrome, Cal. You're drawn to me because I'm the one who'll save your ass. It's not real."

If he didn't know better, the wobble in her voice indicated she feared the words she'd just uttered.

His emotions weren't a result of any kind of misguided psychological thing, though. Sure, Cat was a strong warrior type, there to save him and Sarah. But it was more than that too. "There's no psychosocial phenomenon pushing me to need to be with you, Cat. It's you. Your integrity and drive. The way you put others first. That's the person who I'm getting to know."

She surged up, body stiff with denial. "No. This conversation is done, and I need to go check the perimeter." And she left the cavern.

You pushed too hard, Cal. But instinctively, he'd known she'd needed to unbend.

He glanced back to Sarah, asleep in the back of the cavern, and sighed. He should go after her, but leaving Sarah unprotected was something he wasn't prepared to do. Instead, he hunkered down and waited for her return.

TEN

The sun had risen as Tia reached the top of the rocky outcrop. Staring down, she could see the township in the distance. They probably could have made the last kilometre or two and found somewhere to stay, but her intuition urged caution. She always listened to that.

Well, nearly always.

Otherwise, she would have squashed the interest she had in the man currently guarding Sarah. The very male who'd been in close quarters with her for over a week and whose scent she couldn't banish from her mind, let alone the way he stepped up without question now, having assumed the role of her second without a complaint.

"Concentrate, Tia. You'll get us all killed." The words fluttered away into the atmosphere, and she sighed before turning her attention back to what lay around their present location.

A sense of disquiet gnawed at her. So far, except for a couple near brushes, they'd made their escape with relative impunity. It wouldn't last. Something had to go wrong. Just what and when?

Her mind felt like a scrambled mess. Unloading her sad tale on Cal had been unprofessional. "And you're nothing if not professional, Tia. So why?" He got under her skin, tore back the layers of self-protection she'd wrapped around herself over the years. This one man—a person she'd met less than a week ago and knew so little about—made her spill her guts like this. *Inconceivable.*

She lowered herself so she sat on a rock and rubbed her aching forehead. It seemed to do that a lot right now. Or at least every time she struggled to get back to the matter at hand rather than focusing on him.

"Get your head in the game, girl. They're both counting on you to get them out of here and safely."

She let her gaze drift over the vista. As the day wore on, there'd be more vehicles and people traversing this area. They were almost right beside the road, but the location was best for them to watch and plan.

In the distance, she noted the long fence, the way it stretched out. The checkpoint was on the other side of the town, more extensive than she'd expected. The huts and houses obscured the edges of the town, and Tia bit her lip.

If she'd come here on holiday, no doubt Zabuti would have struck her as colourful and lively. Today that same activity posed a genuine threat to her charges.

She needed to get closer, take a look at the fencing, try to scope out somewhere they could cross.

A car was what she needed—a way to escape the twenty-four-hour cycle of guards and throngs of humanity. The militia didn't know her, of that she was sure. She still kept a wide berth, though, even when they'd travelled to the market. She'd have to slump down, keep her face hidden below her hat. Hell, they likely wouldn't even be able to tell she was a woman.

"And a white woman, out alone in a strange car on the border of Zabuti and Zimbabwe won't stand out like a sore thumb?" Her words echoed. She would, but what other options were there? If she had a way of contacting Cara, maybe she'd take the chance and head into the bustling town. Make contact and arrange some kind of diplomatic passage for the three of them.

Tia scrambled down the rock face and headed toward the cave entrance when the roar of a vehicle caught her attention. She snarled. "Fucking hell. Head in the game, Tia, or it's all over for the three of us."

It was the vehicle she'd seen Vorhoek in earlier, she was sure of it, and a skitter of ice moved down her spine. Tia moved faster, a rush of pebbles and rocks cascading around her, and she slipped and slid her way to the cave. Dashing inside, she tugged the rock she'd found over just in time. *I hope it's enough to hide our location.*

Stupid. Stupid. The word echoed in Tia's mind, and she shook her head. "Vorhoek. Get back to Sarah and wake her. Keep her quiet, though," she muttered forcefully at Cal and snatched up the rifle she'd laid on top of the pack beside the entrance once she'd checked, loading the cartridge.

The vehicle came to a screaming halt, and voices echoed. "Sarah! Where are you, Sarah? Come out and I won't hurt your friends," a man called.

Tia's hands tightened on the rifle, the weight reassuring as she allowed the persona she assumed on patrol to take control. She glanced back at Cal—just a second, but it was enough. "Keep her quiet," she mouthed, and he nodded his understanding.

Her attention was entirely refocused outside, watching Vorhoek and his people searching for them. Once, they came perilously close to their hiding place. She peered through the sight, searching for the golden triangle of neck and hips. A head shot would be efficient, most thought, but she knew damned well a stray breeze or even the temperatures could affect a bullet's trajectory. Better to go for a shot that would kill them, even if it wasn't an immediate kill. That way, they'd be out of the picture, and she could concentrate on the others.

Tia waited; patience was important because once she engaged Vorhoek, his men would know where their hiding place was. There were three of them once more, and they crowded together, hunting for her group, but she could only count on herself. Cal was more emergency backup without her skills and training.

If she fired now, she might kill one, immobilize another, but a third in close contact? That was too high a risk, she calculated.

Time slowed to a crawl.

"I'm going to find you, Sarah. Then I'll kill you. Slit your throat and dance in the pools of blood. Just like jumping in puddles. How does that sound?" Vorhoek yelled.

A muffled whimper told her Sarah had woken and Cal was attempting to keep her quiet.

She'd kill the fucker for the cruelty he was describing. The child was terrified, and Tia could smell it. The ripeness was hopefully obscured by her body and the camouflage they'd hastily erected on their arrival.

"We found the hut, you know. Saw the holes. I know there's an adult with you. I'll kill him too, Sarah. Why don't you come out now and make it easy?"

Tia shut out the rest of the sounds, focusing only on where the men searched. They knew Sarah was holed up somewhere close by but not the exact location.

Something had to give.

If only there were an easy out.

Perhaps there was.

Tia beckoned Cal forward and whispered, "I'm going to do something. It'll be loud and disorientating. Whatever happens, don't look. Just keep going. I need you to get Sarah out of here. Don't let her come back. Get into the town. Find the market and blend in. I'll find you as soon as I can."

She rummaged in her pack, at the bottom where she'd hidden the flash bangs, and pulled one out, then shoved her rifle into the pack before shouldering the weight. They only had one chance, and she looked back to make sure the two of them were ready, packs on their backs and the child's eyes round.

With urgent hand gestures, she indicated they should move to the side, out of view. Then she swept out of the cave, hoping like hell this diversion would work. "Hey, boys, I don't know who the Sarah you're looking for is, but honestly, you suck."

They whirled, and she urged the two out. "The car," she yelled and grabbed her pistols, moving backward in an unsteady retreat.

A crack split the air, and a shower of rock shards filled the heavens, striking her in the face and arm. A sting bloomed where she'd been hit, but Tia ignored it.

Tia growled and squeezed off a round, instinctively aiming for a body shot. One of the guards went down with a scream of pain. He rolled and yelled, and that filled her with hope. *One down, two to go.*

The roar of an engine told her Sarah and Cal had made it to the truck. Satisfaction filled her.

"Hey, boys, did that hurt? Just a little?"

Vorhoek swore.

There wasn't a lot of cover, but she made the best use as he fired again. This time it pinged off farther from her.

"Bad shot!" she bellowed and laughed, ducking down behind a large boulder when the remaining guard aimed and fired.

"Time," she muttered to herself and reached for the stun grenade she'd stashed in her pocket. There were only a few metres between her and the guards, she noted, as she sized up the two left. The guard had little training, and Vorhoek? He was clambering and grunting, making hard work of trying to reach her. An old man in her world, he wasn't fit like she was. That was a check on her side of the equation.

She looked down at the grenade, then up to their location, tugged the pin out, and lobbed the item, turning away and diving down the rocks to the ground.

The rocks jutted out, sharp edges tearing skin, but once the grenade hit, the concussive blast would be worse.

Tia hunched over, covering her ears and hiding her head even as she heard the boom. Her ears were ringing in the aftermath. The blast itself set off a chain reaction in the rocks as she stumbled away with speed, her number one objective.

At least she wasn't blinded, even though she was now effectively deaf until the after-effects wore off, but she belted down the road, moving in a zigzag direction. She was reasonably sure that even if Vorhoek survived, he'd be temporarily blinded for all intents and purposes.

At the outskirts of the town, she slowed, looking for the vehicle, and found it abandoned, keys still swinging in the ignition.

She couldn't blend, not with the military pack on her back and the butt of her rifle exposed, nor the twin sheaths for her pistols. Tia made her way through the thronging masses, scanning left and right for the man and child who were her responsibility.

"Cat!" a voice called, and she whirled, coming face to face with Cal and Sarah.

"Thank God," she said and took the girl's hand. Her gaze met Cal's worried one. "I'm okay." Of course, that was only partially true. She'd bet there was more than one shard of stone embedded in her skin, and her ears still ached. "We need to find somewhere to hole up," she muttered.

Cal nodded. "I found one."

They moved farther into the market, and he tugged her into a doorway. "They'll rent us a room. He's American, and she's Zabutian."

Tia frowned. "How do you know that? They could be sympathisers."

He shook his head and showed her a poster on the wall. A missing person flyer. It carried the likeness of a teen, maybe fifteen or sixteen. "Their son. He was arrested coming home from school, and they said he'd been involved in the anti-militia movement. He disappeared three months ago."

Her lips thinned. It wasn't much, but right now, she needed a break. If this were all there was, she'd take it. But she wasn't a fool. She'd have to keep her wits about her, stay wary and alert.

Cat looked like hell. Blood streaked the side of her face, and bruises were already blooming. She limped slightly, and he'd bet her injuries hurt.

They'd been busy since arriving in the market, Cal dragging Sarah until they found an American voice at an address he half remembered. A few careful questions had paid off, and they'd found this house. The owners weren't renting rooms currently as a general rule, but once they caught sight of Sarah, they'd welcomed him in.

He hadn't missed the poster at the door either.

The door slammed behind them, and the woman's hands flapped with concern. Cat shook her head. "Bathroom?"

The man sized her up, his brow lifting. "We'll look after the girl. No one will know you're here. Bathroom through there." He pointed to a short corridor, and Cal followed Cat to the tiny bathing room.

She dropped her backpack with a sigh and balanced it against the door once he'd shut it.

"Let me see," he demanded, and she began peeling off her stained pants and shirt, revealing miles of skin covered in plain black panties and bra. *At least they aren't camo.* The thought didn't offset the rapid tightening of his body. He'd been more than aware of her curves since the beginning, and it was becoming more and more difficult not to think of her as a woman—a beautiful, perfectly curved, brave woman, epitomizing strength of will and character.

Cal banished that knowledge with difficulty, inhaling deeply, though the scent of her filled him.

"You okay?"

He shook his head at her words. "Yeah, just thinking we should check your injuries."

Her brow lifted. "Well, here they are." She waved her hand along her body, and he swallowed the words that sprang to mind and refocussed. If he didn't.... His hands balled as he resisted the urge to lean in and kiss her.

"Cal?" Her soft words penetrated the fog of lust surrounding him.

"Yeah. Sure." He didn't have to peer closely to examine the damage, though. Her skin was shredded in spots. Legs and arms heavily bruised. Hands abraded and oozing.

"I fell," she said.

Cal rolled his eyes. "That's such a male comment," he muttered, and she laughed.

"I guess it is, Cal. But you have to admit you make a great damsel in distress. I wonder what you'd look like in a skirt."

He grinned. "Hairy. I didn't shave my legs this season."

The laughter died away. "I have a first aid kit in my bag. Pass it over, will you?"

Once more here was a reminder that she was more than just a woman he felt interest in. She was a soldier, here to get Sarah to safety, and he was simply her sidekick. He leaned over and released the clips of her bag, rummaged through until he retrieved a small soft case. "Here," he said.

"Thanks." She ran water in the sink and washed her face, exposing the mess. "There's tweezers in there. I've got a couple bits of rock that need to be extracted."

He unzipped the bag and found the tweezers after donning the latex gloves on top. "Are you a good patient?"

"I'm okay. It's not like it's major surgery. When you're finished, I'll grab the antibiotic ointment and take some painkillers."

An admission of discomfort which had him frowning. "You're going to be okay to keep going?"

She slanted him a look. "We have to be. I don't reckon we've seen the end of Vorhoek or the militia. I need information, and I'm hopeful this couple will help with that. But whatever we find out, we have to be on the road tonight. Any longer and we endanger a lot of lives."

He found three stones, one buried deep in her flesh, and tugged them out. The only sound she made was a hiss. Then he watched as she washed the area thoroughly. "We should wash here, clean our clothes, and get some rest," she said.

He left her there in the bathroom, aware she was stripping down to step under the shower. He imagined water sluicing over the curves he'd sighted while she'd stood there in her underwear. Now his body felt tighter than fucking wire.

Shaking his head, Cal returned to the others. The woman was making Sarah something to eat; after a week of nutrition bars, the scent had him salivating.

"Where you are going, son?" the man, Walter Umbarto, asked.

"We have to get over the border, but the militia is looking for us. Specifically Sarah." He nodded in the child's direction.

Walter gasped. "The woman. She's here to get you both out?"

Cal knew he was asking about Cat's role and nodded in response. "We have to get to Livingstone, but they're looking for us."

The man smiled. "Today could be your lucky day, then. I have a friend who works in the Zambezi National Park. He's due to pop in today. My wife is his sister."

Cal blinked. "What are you suggesting?"

He was aware of Cat walking down the corridor, her pack suspended in one hand. He remembered the weight and shook his head at the memory.

"What's going on?" Cat's gaze was steely as she watched the man's wife, Abidemi Umbarto, who was serving food to both of them.

"Sit down, Cat," Cal said. "Walter and Abidemi can get us to Livingstone."

Her gaze narrowed. "What?" She took the seat Walter vacated.

"Cat, yes? My wife's brother, Afolabi, is a guide at the park. He's coming later today. I can have him take you as far as the gates to the park. There are ways in that no one other than the guards use. I don't think the militia even know they exist."

Cal watched as Cat considered the information Walter had shared. "Why would he do that?"

"Because his son was taken with ours. He's got no love of the militia either. He returned after schooling in America, and they'd rounded up his cattle and seized his parents' property for their own uses."

What the militia has done to this country, Cal thought. No wonder so much of the populace wanted the democracy Sarah's father was here to put in place. He glanced to Cat as she dug into the fried vegetables placed before her.

"He'll drop you on the Kazungula Road, leading into Victoria Falls. He can't take you any farther, but you'd be able to find a ride, I believe." Walter settled into the seat beside Cat.

"I think we should do this," Cal muttered, and Cat closed her eyes as if conjuring scenarios in her head.

"When is he due here?" Cat asked.

"In about three hours. He's going into the national park and stays for one week on-site," Walter answered. "He doesn't work for the park. He's a self-employed guard. Takes tour groups who contact him through the internet. Makes a good steady living from it."

Cat's eyes widened. "Okay, we'll talk to him. If I think it's okay, then we'll take the chance."

Walter's eyes dropped to her pack. "That's a nice-looking Arctic Warfare Rifle. Is it the AW50F?"

She was out of her chair, face tight, and the nerves that had finally settled in Cal's gut started to take wing again.

"What do you know about rifles?"

He grinned. "I was in the military in America for a couple years. Your accent is either New Zealand or Australian. But the rifle I know, so I'm guessing you're an Aussie, right? So is the girl." He nodded to Sarah.

TiA DIDN'T LIKE THAT HE'D ALREADY SIZED THEM UP. JITTERS started somewhere in her belly, but she controlled them. Now wasn't the time to overreact. Instead, she inclined her head at the man.

"Nice to know I've not gotten rusty. Let me explain. My name is Walter Umbarto, and my wife, Abidemi, returned from America seven years ago. I'm a priest. I was born in America, and my parents were Zabutians. My calling gives me a level of protection, as it does my wife. I also served as a padre in the army."

Now his lips turned down in a profoundly unsettling display of anger. "Our son, Ayokunle, was taken from us. We think because he'd been vocal about the militia, and this was the only way they could target us. We think he's still alive, though who knows with them?"

She wanted to reach out and tell him she hoped so, but words and platitudes didn't help in these types of circumstances, so she stayed silent. Besides, she still had a ton more questions to ask.

"My brother-in-law was in school in England when the church sent Abidemi to America to study missionary nursing. We met at church. She needed to come home, and I knew this area of Zabuti desperately needed spiritual guidance. So we returned."

Cat wondered if there was a reason for the sharing. She waited, keeping her whole body still while her damp clothes dried around her body.

"We see first-hand daily the damage the militia are doing to the people here. The people want their freedom. They yearn for democracy, but they daren't raise their heads for fear they'll be attacked. But in America, I could attend college at the expense of the government. I took the opportunity. These days, while I love Zabuti, I don't openly admit my loyalty remains to the American government. And the CIA."

She deflated like a week-old balloon. CIA. Cal. Now it all made sense. "Did they put you on an alert?"

He nodded. "Something like that."

"All right, then. Sarah needs to wash up, and so does Cal. To be honest, I could do with some downtime too. Are they monitoring phones?"

He nodded, and she sighed, aware she wouldn't be contacting Cara from here. Instead, she'd grasp the lifeline they'd been thrown. "All right, Cal? You go shower. Then I'll escort Sarah."

He nodded silently, and she wondered just what was going on in his mind. Was he pondering what Umbarto had said? She knew he was keen to accept the lift through the national park. It was an unlooked-for miracle.

She also wanted to talk to Umbarto privately. Get the lay of the land and find out how much movement there was of the militia across the border. Because borders, especially those gazetted and drawn on paper, could be fluid at times, especially when it came to undemocratic governments.

"Come." He ushered her to a bedroom. "You need to change your clothing. Blending in will be especially important now." He dragged out boxes of what she gathered were donated items.

"Thank you." She riffled through, looking for clothing she could move quickly in. In the end, Tia settled on a pair of jeans and a T-shirt proudly proclaiming her a "bop girl." It sat snugly over her bust. Lastly, she chose a jacket, light but enough to conceal her pistol holster, except to someone looking. She rolled up her pants and shirt and stuffed them down in the pack, lightened a lot now, as they'd been making their way through the bars.

"You weren't regular army, were you, Cat." It wasn't a query, more a statement, and she smiled.

"I can't tell you that, sorry."

He nodded. "I understand. But you're here to keep the child safe. She's the one who went missing from the embassy around twelve days ago."

"Again, no comment." She followed him from the room, having found two more pairs of jeans, this time in Sarah's size, an extra couple of tops, and some clean underwear for both of them. She'd leave Cal to find his own, telling herself she had no idea of his size.

A big fat lie, her brain told her, and she controlled the snort at the thought. She was more than aware of his size, the breadth of his chest, and the way he looked at her. Like she was a dessert he'd enjoy trying.

In other circumstances, she might have given in to the heat that surrounded him. *I may have enjoyed a dalliance or even something more.*

"But that's not on the cards for me," she whispered, and for a moment, she felt a pang of sorrow and regret. Pushing it down was more challenging than she expected.

She settled into a chair in the lounge area. Once Cal returned, she speared him with a glance. "Your watch," she announced and closed her eyes.

ELEVEN

The old truck's tray wasn't comfortable or clean, but it was a ride through the national park. Cal watched as Cat reclined, one arm around Sarah, keeping her safe. The drive in from the township of Urummburta was the most dangerous, Afolabi had informed them.

Cat kept her eyes open, scanning the horizon, her rifle balanced in her lap. She'd made Cal take the position on the other side of Sarah, allowing him to keep her safe if Cat had to act.

Cal wondered if another reason was that she was just as aware of the proximity between them as he was. He'd caught her speculative gaze when he'd returned from his shower, freshly dressed in tight jeans and an even tighter shirt.

He'd cleaned his jeans and stuffed them into the bag she'd given him at the very beginning of their journey. Once they were dry, he'd put them back on, given the discomfort and display that came with the ones he wore.

"Afolabi said the trip takes about two hours," she said, and he nodded.

"While you were hurrying up Sarah, I spoke with him. He said he'd take us to the farthest point of the Kazungula Road he can safely go. It's a short walk into the township surrounding Victoria Falls."

He noted that she once more rubbed the bridge of her nose. "You okay?"

Cat nodded. "Yeah. Just a headache."

Cal frowned. "I thought you took some pain pills for that?"

She fidgeted on the back of the tray and grimaced. "I did. It's just taking a while to deal with."

Now there was silence as they entered the secured area of the park. The area became more grassed than the desert basin they'd been travelling, and he glanced around. The grasses were long and brown, the underbrush heavier in some locations, with knots of trees dotted irregularly.

When Cat handed him the binoculars, he counted lions and elephants grazing and resting, while overhead birds called and other creatures screamed. He could almost forget that right now they were fugitives.

Almost.

About as much as he could forget the woman sitting close to him, with only a dozing child between them.

WAVING OFF THE UTILITY—TRUCK, SHE REMINDED HERSELF— was more than welcome. It had been neither comfortable nor particularly safe, with no seat belts or even seats, only precarious handholds and the bars across the back of the cabin to cling to on the bumps.

But it had been quick and the wildlife spectacular.

Now, faced with a dozing child in Cal's arms and a short march into Victoria Falls, she wondered if they could afford to take the day. Be normal.

Her emotions kicked in and said, *Take the time.* But if she let down her guard, Cat wasn't sure exactly how she'd be able to keep the interest that rolled off Cal in waves at bay. "Hell, I don't know if I want to."

"What?"

She blushed, a wholly unusual behaviour for her. "We should get moving. Maybe there's a hotel room we could rent. Take a break and give Sarah some time to recover before we hit the road one last time."

They trudged up the road, looking for a hotel. Nothing Tia saw met her requirements. They needed to be secure, where she could control who came and went. Biting her lip because Sarah had started whining again, Tia glanced left and right. "There must be a visitor centre near here," she muttered.

They entered the middle of town, and there one was. "Find a café, Cal. Order me a coffee. White, no sugar, and get her something to eat." Splitting up probably wasn't the wisest choice, but she needed a break. Besides, the kid clung to Cal anyway, and the next little bit would be tricky.

Hurrying in, Tia caught one of the workers' eyes and explained she and her boyfriend and daughter had arrived after backpacking into Victoria Falls. Not a total lie. "We're looking for somewhere secluded and exclusive. Good security. Money isn't an issue, but we need transport within the next hour. I want to pay upfront now, so no hassle on arrival. My little girl's pretty well exhausted."

Tia smiled, although the woman frowned. "Of course. There isn't much accommodation available, but I'm sure the private one, right on the falls, may have a suite available." The woman winced, glancing at her apparel. "But it's expensive."

Tia dragged out the Amex she'd secreted in the straps of her pack. Thankfully it was in the name of Catherine Warner, the one she assumed when she needed an identity. "Doesn't matter. Book me a suite. Something with room for the three of us."

It was clear from the woman's gaze she expected Tia's card to decline the payment, and her eyes shot up when it went through without a hitch. "I'll have the car here in one hour," she murmured, suddenly accommodating. Tia wondered for a moment what kind of kickback she got from the transaction, then dismissed it.

Whether it be the father or the government, the client was paying for Sarah's safe retrieval. If this was what it took, it was what she'd do.

On a whim, she turned back. "I also need a hire car. Something comfortable. One-way rental from Livingstone."

The woman nodded. "There are many models…" She dragged out a flyer, and Tia scanned the options.

"I'll take that." She pointed to the full-size SUV. "Give me the highest coverage you've got too." She waited, almost dancing from foot to foot while the woman completed the paperwork. The card would only be good for the mission's period, and she didn't want issues if something did happen to the car. The ability to simply walk away was worth its weight in gold.

"It will be delivered to you tomorrow morning at the lodge. Just see the concierge there."

Tia beat a quick retreat and scanned the road. Three doors away, she spied a coffee shop and entered it. In the very corner, exactly where Tia would have chosen, sat Sarah and Cal. She made her way over and smiled as she took up the empty seat, dropping her pack beside her.

Some of the other diners glanced in her direction, noting the rifle, before returning to their food. "Reckon they think I'm some big-game hunter?"

Cal coughed on his coffee, and Sarah frowned. "Why do you say that? You're not dressed in green and killing an—"

Cal silenced her, and Tia sighed. The child was far too literal. She wondered if they all were. Vanessa had been, and the idea startled Tia. *Is that why I'm so drawn to Sarah? Because she reminds me of Vanessa?* The fact that she even thought of her long-deceased sibling was sobering. Frightening. It meant the life she'd built around her was in serious jeopardy of falling apart.

Her hand shook on the coffee cup. "I've arranged accommodation and a car to be here in"—she checked her watch—"forty-five minutes, and we've got a rental tomorrow morning. We aren't going to walk since we're over the border. We'll drive." And here, Tia infused the words with false cheer. "That way we can deposit this little piece to the meet point"—she rubbed Sarah's hair affectionately—"and return to normal."

It was as if she'd ruined the moment, because Cal's lips turned down and Sarah became silent, drinking the chocolate milkshake delivered to the table.

She kept an eye on the clock. Ten minutes before they were due for pickup, she cleared her throat. "We should get back there."

Exiting the coffee shop, though, Tia had a distinct impression that they were being watched, as the prickle on the back of her neck made itself known.

She turned, scanned the road, but it was busy with tourists of all persuasions. She mentally scolded herself for dropping her guard and ushered the both of them forward and into the information centre, remaining there until the car arrived.

The woman who'd attended to her booking sailed forward, and Tia had a second to realize she was about to call her name. "Wait," she said and hurried over, leaving Cal and Sarah by the front browsing among the brochures. "I don't answer to Catherine Warner much. It's confusing 'cause my parents always called me Cat. If you'd tell the driver that?"

The woman blinked and nodded. "Of course."

No doubt she got lots of these odd types of requests, given how well-heeled many of the tourists wandering up and down the street appeared.

Just as well. "The woman probably thought I was some dero before I waved the Amex around."

"Dero?" Cal questioned.

"Homeless person," Tia explained.

It played on her mind that neither Cal nor Sarah knew her real name and the amount of deception involved in keeping it under wraps. But the truth was if anyone became aware of her real identity, it would curtail her ability to work undercover. *Not going to happen.*

When the driver arrived in a large white van emblazoned with the hotel's name, he called, "Cat, party of three." Exhaling, she ushered the group forward.

The man offered to take her pack, but she waved him off. "Got my rifle in there, and I don't let anyone but me handle it."

He frowned but clearly was used to the vagaries of game hunters and simply left it with her.

The drive was uneventful, though Cat did keep an eye out for vehicles following. There was one that caught her eye, a black SUV that shadowed close for the first few minutes, then veered off. She released a breath.

"Were they following us?"

Cal's question surprised her. She didn't think he was aware, but then he had also become more useful as the trek had worn on. Heaven knew he might even make a good operative in the field. She stopped those thoughts cold. "Umm, no. I don't think so. They've peeled off."

The vehicle entered a driveway and stopped at a manned gate-house. This was the kind of security Tia wanted for the night. Something with guards, guns, and the intelligence and training to use them properly.

The driver called her forward, and Cat rose. "The guards here need to grab a photo so you've got identification. You have to keep this on you at all times. The guards are ex-army, and the hotel is very clear about the guests' safety and security."

"Sure," she answered and stepped out of the van after calling the other two forward. They snapped a photo of her after she presented her passport in the name of Catherine Warner. With identification in hand, they climbed back onto the bus and drove to reception, where she gladly accepted the keys to the suite she'd booked.

TWELVE

Cal wasn't sure what he expected. Indeed not the lush interior they were ushered into. The lobby was deeply carpeted, with vaulted ceilings and heavy dark furniture, and it oozed wealth and luxury. He waited while Cat attended to the formalities, as off-putting as that was, seeing as under normal circumstances that would have been his role. With keys in hand, they climbed into a cart and were en route to their suite.

They entered the rooms, and Sarah squealed. There was a large bedroom and a smaller, obviously child's room, each with their own bathroom. The suite also boasted a sitting and a dining area. Each room was decorated in luxurious style, with plush carpeting and luxury beds.

In the large bedroom, Cat dropped her pack. "Well." She looked around. "Cal, you take the smaller room, and Sarah can stay with me."

Before he could say a word, Sarah marched in. "No, I want the bedroom in there." She stomped her foot.

If the situation wasn't so strange, he might have laughed, but Cat shook her head, crouched down to Sarah, and explained, "You need to stay with me, honey. Just to be safe."

Initially, the little girl seemed sweet, but Sarah had been changed along the way, her lips now set in a mulish thin line. The girl stamped her foot and shook her head. "No. I want my own bedroom."

Cal sighed, realizing that opposition between Cat and Sarah might not be wise. "How about she takes the small room but we leave the doors open? I'll sleep on the lounge."

Cat didn't appear appeased. "I should take the lounge, then, so I can hear—"

"Do you think anyone is going to get to Sarah here? Didn't you choose the hotel because of the security on the grounds?" Cat appeared unconvinced, so he pushed a little harder. They all needed a break from the tension and the highly charged emotional load they'd struggled with. "Come on. It's one night, and you said it yourself. Vorhoek is likely no longer an issue. We've gotten across the border."

Tension oozed from her frame, and she gave in. "I need to check in with my boss first. Stay out here or clean up. Grab a drink from the minibar, but don't leave the suite."

She turned and left them standing there. Cal looked down at the girl, who continued to scowl. "Well, how about a nice soda, then?"

The girl's eyes brightened and she nodded. "Yeah."

Tia closed the door softly and looked at the room. The size of it, the colours, and the furnishings all spoke of wealth. The kind she was wholly uncomfortable with. She'd chosen this hotel—as Cal had pointed out—because it had the best security in the area. Not that she felt overly comfortable. The only thing that would remove the sense of responsibility from her shoulders was when she safely had Sarah back on her way to Australia.

Sarah. The little girl reminded her so much of Vanessa these days. When necessary, Sarah had accepted Tia's rules, but now that there was a sniff of freedom, her eyes sparkled, and she wasn't afraid to let Tia know what she wanted. Or didn't.

Running a shaking hand over her forehead, Tia attempted to push the memories back until the layers she'd built over the years were back in place. Forgetting was the best way to cope. She knew that from experience, because memories were more than inconvenient in the field. They were also dangerous when they played with your head.

Whirling, Tia reached for the phone, the number memorized, and dialled the hotline Cara had devised for checking in.

"Alathea Forestry." Leonie—Leonie Samuels—had answered the call, just like they all took turns doing. It was a system that worked for them on the odd occasion they needed to report their location.

"Hey. Cat here. Victoria Falls is lovely this time of day. I just wanted to let my sister know the family is well."

For a moment, there was only the clicking of keys. "Of course. I'll pass that on." The line went dead, and Tia replaced the handset.

She'd done all she could for the moment. Tia walked to the large glass doors at the end of the room. She'd already scanned the exit points in her quick initial check. One through this door, another to the front, and a sliding door to the patio abutting the seating zone at the suite's rear.

Glancing over the grounds, she sighed. No one in sight, though the grassed area spanned a long way. Over the tops of the trees, she caught sight of what appeared to be a security tower. "I'll check that with my glasses later," Tia murmured.

She noted a terrace downstairs, having caught sight of the edge of the paving and the lights fitted above. It would be lit all night long, likely.

She tested the slider's door jamb and was satisfied that it was sturdy, the glass itself reinforced with almost non-existent filaments woven through it. Not bulletproof but it would give them time to alert security in the case of an attempted entry event. "Good."

There were no other windows in the room that she could see, so she marched into the other bedroom, checked the window, and was pleased to note the same glass installed.

The patio slider also had the same latch system and glass, reassuring her that it was a well-maintained facility. Tonight, they could rest in peace, especially once they'd engaged the security system on the doors.

Once they were all in the lounge, Cat looked at Cal and Sarah. "We should order room service for tonight. There's no need for us to leave here."

Sarah opened her mouth to complain, but Cat shook her head, and Cal nodded his agreement. "The less we're seen, the better. But I should call in my whereabouts."

Tia shook her head. "My people will do that for you." His frown told her he had questions, but she smiled at him. "We can discuss all that later on."

She knew damn well that the situation had to be chafing for him. Not emasculating but difficult to accept. He may not have been a physical operative as such, but he was a man. They were usually in charge, and she'd seen the disastrous fallout that could come hard on the heels of a woman taking control. But now wasn't the time to prosecute that argument, she reminded herself. Instead, she strode over to the cabinet, where there was an artfully displayed range of flyers on a silver tray.

Flipping through, she noted tours, adventure safaris, and finally the dine-in menu.

"Sarah, is there anything you don't like?"

Tia realized after Sarah rattled off a list that she should have just ordered. Instead, she checked against a list of options. "Okay, steak for you. Cal?"

"Some fish would be lovely. It's been a while, and I'm always wary of what's on offer in landlocked countries."

She couldn't help but laugh a little at the words. She knew what Cal meant. For herself, the only option was steak—a big juicy slab, cooked to medium and piled with fries and vegetables. High calorie, it was true, but protein and carbs were her friends right now.

Once they'd ordered, she sent Sarah for a bath, and only when she was sure the girl was busy in the bathroom did she pin Cal with her gaze. "You've got questions, and while I will answer them, now is not the time. We'll wait until Sarah is asleep, and then we can talk."

He nodded. Whether that was enough to settle his aggravated nerves, Tia didn't know, but for now, it would have to do.

THIRTEEN

Cal waited, a glass of wine in his hand. Cat had agreed that one drink was acceptable, and the shiraz's rich ruby ended the night perfectly.

He wondered what Cat was thinking as she nursed her soda water, waiting for Sarah's breath to settle into the steady rattle that warned them she'd finally dropped into a deep sleep.

The lounge was shrouded, the lights dimmed, and the curtains were drawn after Cat had "made her rounds," as she called them, checking every window and door and setting the security system for the evening.

She was rimmed with light, and it outlined the curves of her body, the finesse of her bone structure. The feelings Cal had tried hard to keep to himself had grown over the last few days, and here, relaxed with a glass of wine, he wondered what she'd do if he kissed her.

"Cat?"

She turned, a question on her face.

"I...." How did a man open this kind of discussion with a woman like her? Could she read the interest he felt?

She shifted closer. "What's wrong, Cal?"

"Lots. Too much and not enough." The words jumbled in his brain.

She frowned. "I don't understand."

He leaned in, taking a chance and merely acting. When his lips met hers, the touch was soft. Her lips were pliant beneath his, the whisper of her breath minty and inviting.

When her mouth opened beneath the caress, he pushed deeper, his tongue surging into the moist cavern of her mouth.

She moaned, and he reached out, sliding his hands to her waist and hauling her closer. Their bodies rested against each other, and the touch was electric.

Her arms found their way around his shoulders, her fingers tangling in the length of his hair.

It felt like coming home.

She pulled away, chest heaving, eyes sparkling, and lips swollen. "I.... Don't."

She slid her hands to her hair while her cheeks bloomed a dark pink of embarrassment.

"Don't what, Cat? Don't kiss you? Don't want you?" He leaned in, knowing this time she wouldn't allow the interlude to continue. "It's too late, Cat. I'm captivated by you."

Her eyes closed, and she sucked in a breath, unsteady and rasping. It both filled Cal with hope and tore him apart.

"I'm an operative, Cal. My job is to keep people like you and her safe. I don't get the luxury of falling for anyone. I don't have a normal life where the hopes of a white picket fence and forever count."

"I don't care, Cat."

"That's not even my real name!" Her voice shook with emotion, but he couldn't control his smile. He wondered just how many others she'd made the admission to. Likely none, if he was reading her correctly.

"Then what is it?"

Her eyes opened, the brown depths filled with regret. "I can't tell you, Cal. It puts too many people at risk. Too many lives, and I can't...." It appeared she struggled for words. "I won't do that. When I joined the force, I promised I'd give my all to the group. I stand by that. I made a vow, Cal. One I can't just sideline because I've fallen for some guy."

He blinked and wondered if she'd considered the importance of the words she'd just uttered. "You've fallen?"

She blanched. "Work. This is all work, Cal. It has to be. The little girl in there depends on me to keep her safe and get her home."

"But that won't be forever, Cat."

He watched as she fought for control of her emotions, her hands clenching and releasing, her body tensing as she withdrew from him emotionally. "No. But then there'll be someone else, Cal. Another person who needs my skills. Another person to kill, or a mission to take me away."

She believed that, he realized. That she was only part of something bigger, with no value of her own. He reached out, caressed her cheek while she watched him. "You discount yourself and your needs. One day, you'll be ready. One day, you'll see that walking alone through life leaves you empty and cold. On that day, I'll still be waiting for you."

He retreated from the room, aware they both needed some space between them.

FOURTEEN

Cal had left Tia alone with thoughts that roiled through her mind, but she desperately wanted to embrace the quiet.

If only it were that simple. In the moment where he'd held her against him, she'd felt the depths of his desire for her. Tia knew she could attempt to write off the connection between them as lust.

Maybe that's precisely what you should be doing, her mind whispered. There was a large bed, the child was asleep, and they were as secure as they could get. Close the door, ride him hard, and enjoy a night of no-holds-barred passion.

The thought of sex and Callum Gallagher had her body almost singing the "Hallelujah" chorus. Except she couldn't, the angel on her shoulder reminded her.

During the last week, she'd come to respect him. To bed and then leave him when this was all over reeked of taking advantage. Not at all her style. "Besides, that's not how this job goes. Getting involved with a client is just the way to an early grave," she told herself.

The devil on her shoulder whispered, *But he's not the client or the job.*

The angel countered with *But he's here helping with the job. So, keep arm's length.*

Instead, she'd suck it up. File those hot kisses away for long nights when she could have a glass of wine or a beer—or three. She could take the memories out, let them warm her when the cold of her isolation invaded her body and BOB didn't satisfy the physical need.

With that in mind, she checked on the child again. Asleep. Tia pulled Sarah's door to but not closed. She'd open it again when ready to sleep so she'd hear any prowlers, though her intuition said they wouldn't get to them tonight. Staying another night would undoubtedly increase the risk, but with luck, by this time tomorrow, they'd be on their way to their home or with the plans in place to get Sarah and her father on a plane. Once she'd handed the child over, she'd be free to arrange transport back to San Diego.

Scooping up the phone, she called the concierge desk. "Can you advise which airlines fly direct from Livingstone to Sydney in the next few days?"

The man coughed and spluttered. "There's none at the moment, Ms. Warner. We don't know when that will be changed. The only flights to Sydney currently are out of Lusaka, the capital."

Stunned, she looked at the receiver. "Since when?"

"Last week. All flights to Australia were cancelled from Livingstone. But there is plenty of availability from Lusaka. We've changed several guests' bookings in the last couple days. Is there something I can assist with?"

"Uhh, no. Thank you." Tia replaced the receiver and stared at it.

All her planning, working on getting them to Livingstone. "Fucking bastards," she whispered. Had they worked out where they were hiding? Did that compromise Sarah's safety?

A strong hand slid over her shoulder.

"What?"

Tia whirled around, her body ready and tense, hands raised to ward off an attack.

"Whoa," Cal murmured, moving slightly back.

With a whoosh of released breath, Tia's muscles relaxed.

She hadn't even heard Cal approach, lost in her fury. *Fucking hell!* She was mucking up on every front. Letting her emotions cloud her thinking. That was dangerous.

Tia refocussed. They'd been hoping she'd not make plans. Not check.

If she hadn't, they would have caught them, likely at the airport. Taken the kid. Her guts twisted at that thought. It wasn't just that she felt responsible now. She genuinely liked Sarah. She had spunk and character.

She sighed. "Change of plans. Tomorrow we head for Lusaka."

"Why?" The quiet acceptance underscored his trust in her, and Tia closed her eyes for a moment, sucking in the strength.

"They've cancelled all flights from Livingstone to Sydney. In the last week." She let that hang for a moment so he'd grasp the import of her words. "We have to head to Lusaka. What can you tell me about it?"

She felt the moment he released her, the loss of touch a sharp jab at her psyche. She listened as he padded away, the quiet pop as he poured her another soda.

"Lusaka is the capital city of Zambia. It's a large urban town. Growing with new buildings going up. It declared independence from Rhodesia in 1964. It has somewhere in the region of 1.8 million and is known for producing textiles, shoes, cement, and processed foods. It's also been instrumental in homing anti-colonial organizations."

She blinked at him. "What was that about a walking encyclopedia?" Tia sank into one of the single chairs.

He laughed, obviously remembering their earlier conversation. "I was based there for several months before being seconded to Zabuti, Cat. I needed to know those kinds of basic facts."

"You haven't ever opened up much about your life pre-CIA."

He handed her the soda water. "I told you about my family. Where I grew up."

"Tell me how you ended up in the CIA first. We'll get to the rest afterward."

He scooped up his drink and settled into the chair opposite. "You know I grew up in Santa Clarita. Initially, I thought city politics would interest me. So, when I finished school, I went to college, as any good son does. I chose political sciences, thinking that would give me a decent grounding. I was just finishing when I got the tap on the shoulder. The recruiter suggested that I had a feel for the current climate, asked if I had considered working for the government."

Tia inclined her head. "What exactly does that mean?"

"That's the question I asked upfront. He said they needed people in other countries to keep their fingers on the pulse. I'd already shown I was savvy, according to them, in politics, as I'd been involved in the student political body during my time at UC."

When she blinked, he laughed.

"University of California, in Berkley."

"Ahhh. So then what?"

"I did my training and was initially sent to Hong Kong, then New Zealand. They like us to start in 'soft' locations, as they call them. Hong Kong not so much, but New Zealand, now that was nice. I even got to Brisbane a few times. I liked it. Lots of land and open space. Not like at home. This reminds me of Australia in some ways."

"Do you enjoy your job?"

The question was clearly a surprise from the way his eyes widened. He considered it for a moment. "Yes and no. I like to travel and meet people. I enjoy seeing the world and being able to sum up the situation. The intrigue not so much. In Hong Kong, there was a lot of unrest. Given the political climate since it was handed back to the Chinese, it's unstable. I can't see that changing any time soon, though. Things are going to get worse. You could see the hallmarks years ago."

Tia nodded. "Yeah. I was on a mission years ago. Had to transit through Hong Kong, and while I enjoyed the bustle, I could read the place was on edge then."

"What about you? Where did you live after your family...?" His words trailed off, but she knew what he was asking.

She smiled. "Lots of places. I was in foster care, and they wanted to keep me in the general area. Didn't want to disrupt my schooling too much was their thinking. I hated school because everyone knew my story, but I did okay academically. I was pretty good at sports and trained almost constantly because it let me forget. To be more than the sum of my story, I guess. I did consider being an athlete, but I wanted more. I wanted to get away from where I lived. I wanted a life untainted by my history. When I turned seventeen, I applied to the government for permission and received the okay to apply to the army. I left Queensland three days after I finished high school. Never went back."

"We both outgrew our beginnings, it seems." He smiled, and it was soft and full of understanding. It tugged at her.

"You wanted to discuss other stuff, though. So now's good. Sarah's asleep."

"Vorhoek?"

Biting her lip, Tia considered the situation. "I know I shot one of the guards. The other one and Vorhoek were on the hill when I got away. I can't say for certain if they're dead or not. There's a better than even chance he escaped and was just injured or at least affected by the blast. I only used a small grenade."

"So, we're not safe, then, are we?"

Tia scrubbed a hand over her face. "It's not quite that simple. If Vorhoek was in contact with the militia's head, then chances are they're still looking for us. If Vorhoek got away, he might have been able to tip off the forces to us being in that town. The question is how far the tendrils reach. You'd know that better than me."

His face tightened. "As I said, Zambia houses many of the anti-colonial bodies. There are also facets of the militia and sympathisers. So, I guess that means we have to be on our guard still?"

She nodded. "Yes. The car will be here by seven in the morning. We get down and in. Then we drive to Lusaka. It's the only way we're going to get out of this mess."

FIFTEEN

Cat threw the keys in Cal's direction. "You know the region, so you're the driver. You are a decent driver, aren't you?"

"Yeah. The CIA likes its people to be well rounded. They insisted on sending us through a defensive driving course. Dodging tanks and unstable political leaders are high on my ability list."

Cat laughed and unfurled the information book she'd picked up from the concierge desk. Not that she'd made any plans.

"Where are we headed tonight? Hotel?"

She shook her head. "The guy at the desk asked me that, and I said I didn't know, that we'd wing it. As far as the militia knows, we're looking for a way out of here. If they come to the staff here, they've got no information on where we're headed."

He frowned. "Last night, you asked about flights to Sydney."

Cat gazed out the window. "Yeah. If anyone asks about flights, it won't take much to work out Lusaka is our destination."

"We're going to Livingstone," Sarah piped up from the back seat.

"Not now, Sarah. We have to go to Lusaka instead. How's the book?"

"Yeah, it's okay."

Cat had purchased an e-book reader and downloaded fifteen books to it immediately on leaving the shop.

Cal was pretty sure Cat hoped it would keep Sarah occupied and out of their conversations. With the new destination in mind, it probably paid not to reveal too much. He agreed. Sarah was still a child—one who'd come through a scary experience, undoubtedly, but she wasn't necessarily capable of keeping the information to herself.

At least the car handled well, had air conditioning, and Cat noted her pack fit on the back seat, not in the trunk. "Easy reach for the rifle," she'd pointed out as they left the safety of the hotel grounds.

The mirth ceased as they joined the queue to make the crossing from Zimbabwe to Zambia.

"Whatever is said, Sarah, remember I'm your mother, and your name is Sarah Warner. Cal is Callum and my boyfriend," said Cat. Concern filled her voice, but in the end, they sailed through with only a few questions about the rifle and pistols. All had the required paperwork in the name of Catherine Warner.

"Dear God, I was worried for a few minutes there," Cal muttered as they drove away from the checkpoint.

"You and me both, Cal. I've still got one stun grenade in the backpack, and I'm not sure they'd be too happy knowing I'm carrying one of those," Cat answered.

After the first hour, Sarah's "are we nearly there's" started, and Cal wondered how his sisters coped with more than one child. Sarah was pretty good, but she was clearly tired of the long hours of travelling at the heart of it.

They stopped for a quick break at midday. The pre-packed lunch box Cat had organized—yet another sign that she'd taken as many variables as possible into account—consisted of sandwiches, fruit, and cold drinks.

Cat insisted they keep the breaks to a minimum but drove for a stretch before he regained the wheel at just after three in the afternoon.

"We're about two hours out. We should choose a hotel," Cal

urged, and Cat agreed, fishing a cell phone from her pocket. He glanced at it, then back at her. "How long have you had that?"

She smiled. "Since this morning. I grabbed it while you two were piling into the car. I purchased a Zambian SIM card so I'd be able to use it." Then she dug a tourist booklet from her bag, studying it.

Tia stared at the brochure, willing something, anything that met their needs to pop up. Nothing came to mind, and she growled.

"What's wrong, Cat?"

"There's nothing suitable. We need to get Sarah somewhere safe, and I don't know how when I can't find an apartment, hotel, or even a villa with adequate security." The itch on the back of her neck, the one she'd noticed in the last hour, increased.

Once more, she chanced a look at the road behind them. Two cars followed—one a dark, heavily tinted SUV, the other an older beaten-up Ford.

Her money was on the dark SUV if she had to choose between them for someone tracking. "Hey, Cal?"

"Yeah?"

"You see the car behind us? With the dark tinting? The SUV?"

"Sure," he answered, then glanced in her direction. "Are they following us?"

"Could be. How long have you noticed them there?"

"Since we got back in the car from lunch."

That gelled with her understanding too. It meant that choosing a hotel or somewhere to stay was now of vital importance. If they were being followed, and she couldn't at this time be sure of that, then they'd have compatriots likely alerted via phone. They'd be watching for the vehicles.

She calculated the variety of road choices based on the built-in

GPS in the car. "Cal, how good is your relationship with the ambassador?"

Suspicion filled his face. "Good. You want to go to the American embassy with an Australian child?"

She bit her lip. "Might be a wise option."

He shook his head. "It's not that simple, Cat. Getting me in is enough of a task, but you and Sarah? I don't think that's possible."

"There's not a full embassy for Australia in Lusaka, Cal. Only an honorary consul, and that isn't enough to protect her. That's the problem with this option. If I thought we could get a ride through to the airport and her father would be able to meet me there, I'd do that. But I can't. My instructions are clear, though. I've got to keep her safe until I can hand her over." Frustration built in her voice. "I can't put a kid on a plane without an adult, and getting you a visa is near impossible in the short amount of time I have. I'm running out of options."

He grunted. "I know of a place. It's not as secure as last night, but it's a private residence. Used by embassy staff. I reckon I could get us in there."

She grunted. "Security?"

"Provided by the embassy."

She tossed it around in her mind. It wasn't perfect, but with no other options right now, she'd take it. "How do I contact them?"

He grinned, though she didn't miss the white lines bracketing his mouth and eyes. "You don't. I do."

He reeled off a number, and she dialled, then held the phone up for him to speak.

"You've reached Helen's phone. I'm busy right now, but if it's urgent, I'll get back to you" came a sultry voice, and a burn began in Tia's gut.

"Hey, Helen, it's Cal Gallagher. I've got a situation and need your help. I need access to the secured apartment tonight. I'm travelling with some people who need a safe place to bunk down. Call me back on this number."

She hung up when he finished, and he hit the steering wheel. "Dammit. Normally if she can't answer, her assistant does. I don't—"

The phone rang, and Tia answered. "Hello?"

"Uh, hi, this is Helen. I'm looking for Cal Gallagher." It was the sultry voice from the answering service. She held the phone back up so Cal could talk.

"Hey, Helen. I've got a situation."

"I heard. I also know you've been working with the Zabutian embassy on something. Is it to do with that?"

"Yeah. Sort of. Look, we need a secure location for tonight. One of the apartments in the building would do, if you could swing it?"

Tia waited through the silence, interrupted only by the click of a keyboard.

"Hmm, I have one. The two-bed on the top floor. I can meet you at—"

"The building would be best, Helen. We may or may not have grown a tail."

"I see. Are they American citizens, by chance?"

"No—"

Tia dragged the cell phone back. "I'm under engagement to the US military, however. Contact Cooper McDowell, and he'll vouch for Cat."

"Aaaahhhh...." The word held a depth of meaning.

Cooper was her contact when necessary in the military world and would vouch for her. But anyone working in the embassies around the world would know Cooper's name. It was her entrée into places she usually wouldn't have access to, and no one questioned what Cooper said.

"Fine. How long until you arrive? I'll make sure I'm downstairs to wave you in. Registration, colour, and type of vehicle?"

Tia rattled off the information. Once that was complete, she hung up, then checked on Sarah, who'd fallen asleep with the activity book she'd grabbed at the same time as the e-book reader.

"I'll bet she'll be pleased to see her father again," muttered Cal.

"Yeah," Tia said, then turned back to the front. "So long as we can stay alive."

~

Cal drove slowly, the crowds of people going home in Lusaka's central business district slowing them down. The only thing that made him feel better was that the car that had been following them was also in the same boat.

"How much longer do you think?" Cat's face betrayed her concern, one he shared.

"Once we get off this main road, we're less than ten minutes from the apartments," he answered.

The problem was that it was ten minutes longer where they could be targets. He read that on Cat's face while her hands stayed close to her pistols. She'd already unbuckled her seat belt. "Just a precaution," she'd announced.

As they approached the building, he pointed it out to Cat.

"Drop me here, but don't stop the car," she announced, and he frowned, slowing the vehicle as Cat ordered.

He didn't understand her instructions but followed them none-theless. She grabbed the handle of the door and hurled herself out. In the rear-view mirror, he watched as she righted herself, gripping her pistols. His attention focussed back on the building, and he watched as Helen waved her tag in front of the roller door, angling the car to the driveway as the security gate rose.

Bam! He felt the contact from the car behind. "Dammit!"

Sarah cried out, and he jerked the wheel, cutting the corner and speeding down the ramp.

SIXTEEN

Acting on instinct, Tia shoved the woman, Helen, out of the way as three men jumped from the first vehicle.

Tia expected the combatants to act—hell, it was why she'd had him drop her—but this wasn't quite what she thought would happen.

"Fuck," she muttered. "Get the hell out of here," she yelled at the woman.

Shots echoed, and Tia threw herself across the civilian, feeling the bite of the bullet through her leg.

Her mind blanked from the pain for an instant before practice took over.

The sudden shock fuelled the adrenalin coursing through her system.

She levered herself up, raising a pistol, her body acting like a well-oiled machine. Instinct had her squeezing the trigger, and Tia watched as one man jerked on impact. The plume of scarlet told her the hit was successful. He went down. *One shot. One target. Two more to go.*

Tia rolled off Helen. "Run," she screamed at the cowering woman but didn't have time to check if she did.

Her gaze darted sideways and she took in the next man, advancing on him. There was no cover, and she hissed. Her body moved automatically now, the other hand rising, ready to address the threat.

The trigger reacted to the squeezing of her finger, and another boom filled the air.

Wails and sirens echoed as she took a second out. The man screamed as he hit the floor before he could return fire.

She glanced to the third. The man spun, and she could finally see his face.

Vorhoek.

Fuck! He survived the attack on the hill.

His face was a study in fury, red and sliced up from the rock explosion. Tension and hate radiated from him in wild and undulating waves.

"So, you're the fucking bitch who's got the child," Vorhoek snarled.

He advanced, and though Tia was trying vainly to ignore the pain in her leg, it bloomed and pulsed. She was bleeding heavily if the greyness in her vision was anything to go by.

I must hold on. This isn't going to end well if I can't beat Vorhoek.

He came closer, his gaze on her leg, and a smile split his face, sharp white teeth against his sun-darkened skin, eyes shining with mad hatred. "That'll probably do the job for me"—he indicated the injury—"but let's finish it anyway. Then I'll get the little one and gut her like a pig."

Tia kept her mouth closed and looked for an opening. Hand-to-hand wasn't her strongest suit, but she could hold her own. But what could she use? Tia braced, and once he was close enough, she kicked up, wobbling to remain standing while aiming for his balls.

He laughed and danced away, but not before he got a strike in on her injured leg.

Her gaze blanked while fire erupted in her brain.

"Is that the best you've got?" Vorhoek taunted.

She raised the pistols, but there wasn't one or even two of the man. Her brain was haywire. Where to aim? Which Vorhoek was real?

Gritting her teeth, Tia watched—too slowly as he spun too close and too fast. The blood she was losing made her brain sluggish.

He moved in, quick as a snake, his balled fist making contact with her face, and she flew back, slamming into the ground.

She groaned, but the training kicked in again, as the bite of the knife in her boot reminded her there was more than one way to finish it.

Tia jackknifed up, though she felt a bit of nausea, grabbing the handle of the stiletto as she moved and tugging it from her boot.

"Hmm, resourceful little slut, aren't you?" He laughed and lunged, but Tia had noted the way he telegraphed his move and drew away, so his swipe didn't connect.

His foot came up, and she cried out as it crashed into her knee, the crack resounding along with the bloom of pain. She flew through the air, tears leaking from her eyes as her body shrieked.

The sound of footsteps had her looking up. Cal. On the steps.

Then a sudden intrusion, the wet sucking sound of flesh tearing before metal. It sank deep into her belly, and she screamed. Vorhoek's face came close against hers. "I win," he said.

Then a final boom echoed.

The grey deepened, turned black.

Tia ceased to exist.

SEVENTEEN

Cal paced the corridor of the hospital, not that they'd tell him anything. Helen had roused the ambassador, and he'd pulled strings. Cal didn't care what strings so long as Sarah's father made an appearance and Cat pulled through the surgery.

He'd seen her on the gurney. The grey tinge to her skin, the way they worked over her.

The little girl sat in the waiting room, surrounded by the ambassador, Helen, and three guards, but right now, that was of little interest as far as he was concerned while Cat's life was on the line.

Voices echoed, and suddenly a man, trailed by three more of the ambassador's guards, entered the small room.

"Daddy!" Sarah was up, running and jumping into her father's arms.

"Sarah! Oh, baby, I was so worried. But why are we here?" He sounded confused and dazed. "You're okay, aren't you, honey?"

Cal watched distantly as Matthew Berding patted his daughter all over. He cleared his throat, waiting for Berding to focus on him. "She's fit and well. Cat saw to that."

The man glanced up. "So why are we here, then? I'm sure you

didn't just pick this location out of a hat to use as a meet point?" Now, reunited with his daughter, the haughty diplomat demeanour came to the fore.

"No. The operative, Cat, is in surgery. She nearly died getting your daughter to safety, sir. We're waiting to see if she pulls through." Bitterness coated his voice, but he was unable to restrain it. The man didn't care about Cat. She'd only been useful long enough to save his daughter, but now she was surplus to his needs. Expendable.

"Oh. Well...." Berding frowned.

The ambassador stepped forward. "I'm pleased we were able to reunite you two. We should head for the embassy, though. I promised your prime minister and foreign secretary both that I'd personally attend to your safety." Without a further word, the ambassador and his guards ushered the diplomat and child from the waiting room, leaving Cal alone with Helen.

"You're worried about her. She means a lot to you personally," Helen said, and for the first time, he looked up to see the way she watched him. "Cal?"

Though they'd had a personal dalliance in the past, she'd become a good and close friend. "I... I care, Helen. I think I love her, but she's...." He swallowed the lump lodged in his throat. *How do I quantify my fears? She's larger than life. Strong but also fragile.*

"She's special, then." Helen spoke quietly, and he realized she also felt the echoes of his emotions.

She cared for him. He'd never noticed it before. It humbled but also hurt because he couldn't return her affections. His heart was no longer his. It belonged to the woman in the room beyond.

His gut clenched. *What if Cat doesn't make it through? What if she... dies?* His throat closed at that thought, and he dragged in a rasping breath, dropping to a seat and slumping with his head in his hands.

Time passed, and he waited, feeling the tick of every second that went by.

The doors to the surgical suite finally whooshed open, and he jerked out of his chair and turned.

The male nurse looked haggard. "We don't know at this time if she's going to pull through. She lost a lot of blood, her knee will need reconstruction, and the knife wound nicked a lung. There's a chance of infection too."

Cal staggered to the chair, grabbed the arm. "You don't know...?"

"She's still under the knife, sir. We're doing our best."

Glancing up at the man's face, though, Cal feared their best wasn't good enough.

Helen took Cal's hand. "How much longer do you think?"

The man shrugged. "You should go home. We'll let you know when she's out of surgery and in recovery." Then he retreated through the swinging doors.

Cal was sure his life would never be the same again, especially if Cat didn't pull through. Without her breathing and alive somewhere in the world.

He thought about the things she'd said, about family, then turned to Helen. "I need you to contact Connor. Have him make contact with her boss. Let them know."

Feeling like an old man, he stood and moved with Helen to the door.

"I'll do that, Cal, but don't give up. If she's half as strong-willed woman as you, she'll pull through."

It had to be enough.

EIGHTEEN

Was it day?

Was it night?

Time had no meaning in the place where Tia remained. A prisoner of pain, limbs heavy and useless. Her tongue was swollen, her mouth dry.

She recognized the lights. Sounds. She wanted to reach out, but before she could, it faded once again.

Opening her eyes was a chore. Her throat ached, and her mouth was dry, but she couldn't talk because something was in her airway, obstructing her ability to swallow. Choking her. She started to cough.

Before the blackness overwhelmed her again, she heard voices crying out, "Sedation!"

A third time she swam up through the waves that wanted to suck her down into emptiness. The pressure held her still. Straps keeping her in place while a kind voice told her it would be okay. To remain calm. It soothed the beast—the rapid heartbeat—raging in her chest. The *beep beep beep* of a monitor echoed in the quiet.

Soft fingers touched her forehead, but heat seared her from the inside out.

"Hot," Tia croaked, and the nurse sucked in a deep breath.

"I know, Cat. We're working to bring the fever down. You just have to cooperate."

The sting of something entered the flesh of her arm, and it brought tranquillity while she floated away on a soft cloud.

Opening her eyes was hard. They fluttered as she fought to attain consciousness. Finally they flicked open, though there was a weight to the awareness.

Beeping sounds and the stink of disinfectant and bleach permeated the air. "Hospital," she croaked.

"Yes, Cat. Good to have you back in the land of the living," a voice she didn't know sang near her head, and she made a move to turn toward it. "No, you stay still. I'm just taking your observations. Then I'll come down, and we can chat."

Tia blinked. "Thirsty," she said, though her voice was little more than a whisper.

"No wonder, dear."

The sound of swishing fabric told her the woman had moved. A straw slid against her lips, and Tia opened her mouth. She sucked the water, letting it slide down the back of her throat. Not nearly enough to ease the burn that remained there, but a start. "Where... am I?"

"A private hospital in Lusaka, dear. You were transferred two days ago, once released from the Intensive Care Unit."

"And who... who are... you?" It was challenging to get a sentence out.

"Luisa. I'm your day nurse, and Lenny will be in soon. She'll stay with you through the night, but now that you're finally awake, we can get the doctors to look at removing some of the things you're attached to. Like the catheter." The woman's voice was English.

Tia blinked, confusion still uppermost in her mind, but she fought to overcome it.

The word didn't make sense for a moment. "Catheter?"

"Mmm-hmmm. For urine output. Now, then, how's your pain?"

The fog was descending. "What?" Exhaustion sapped her, and she panted. She closed her eyes while her body betrayed its weakness by trembling.

Her stomach felt like it was about to explode, and her leg and knee radiated pain. "Fu... cking aw... ful," she answered finally, and the nurse, Luisa, laughed.

"Yes, I can imagine it is. I'll just get the pain injection. Oh, and you have a visitor. He's been here every day since you were admitted. He sent these lovely flowers for you." She pointed to a vase full of roses in front of her on a sliding table. "I'll send him in, though he can only stay a moment."

She disappeared from view, and Tia closed her eyes.

"Cat?" She knew that voice. Cal.

"Cal? What. Are. You. Doing. Here?" Every word was an effort, but she pushed them out.

The job's done, isn't it? her brain slyly offered.

He moved into view, unshaven and dishevelled. "I was worried about you." He took her hand and squeezed. "You made it. For a while, they didn't expect you to."

Was that bright sheen in his eyes tears?

Before she could be sure, Luisa bustled back in. "Well, now you're going to have to leave because I'm going to give Cat something for the pain, and she'll sleep again. If you wait outside, I'll join you soon."

She ushered Cal out, then returned, slid something into the IV hanging above the bed.

Tia's eyes grew too heavy to stay open once the cooling drugs entered her system, and she let sleep claim her.

~

CAL HATED THE NEED TO RETREAT.

The woman in the other room, pale, skin near translucent, was not just the dangerous fighter he'd passed so much time with.

She was the woman he loved.

That knowledge had come during the fight that nearly stole her life.

Cat shoved out the door, and Helen raised the screen. He drove through the building. He didn't pause for a moment because he knew in that split second precisely what he had to do.

He heard her voice, the scream: "Run!" Knew she was sending Helen to safety, but he'd heard the shots. His gut had clenched hard. Was he too late?

Grabbing Sarah from the back seat, he shoved the car door closed and raced as fast as he could manage for the stairs.

"Stay here," he bellowed at Sarah, shoving her through the secure, bulletproof door. They wouldn't get to Sarah so long as she stayed inside. "Don't open for anyone except Cat and me. Or Helen, okay?" Feeling as if he were wasting time, he took the extra second to wait for her reply.

Sarah watched him, her eyes wide open with fear as she nodded.

Helen met him at the door as it slammed behind him.

"She's.... He's going to kill her. Do something!" Helen's fear washed over him. His hands moved instinctively, curling around the butt of the gun.

A primal surge of power overwhelmed him. "Look after Sarah." He threw the door open once more and waited for Helen to step within the room.

The scene before him was shattering. Men dead on the ground, blood and brain matter spattered on the road. It was Cat he sought, though, and his horrified gaze settled on Vorhoek, watching as he shattered her knee and she went flying with an "Oomph." The large knife in her hand spun away on the path. He felt the impact as she slumped on the ground, bloodied and beaten.

Vorhoek scooped up the knife from where it lay on the grass, his grin gleeful. Before Cal could move, Vorhoek lunged, sliding it deep into Cat's belly.

"Noooo!" His scream had the man looking up, and Cal's finger squeezed, his aim true.

The man jerked as the bullet landed in his chest, red blooming and pulsing even while the boom of the gunshot died away.

He needed to check Cat, but Vorhoek first, his brain urged.

The man lay still, eyes open, and while a dribble of blood escaped through the side of lips as he whispered, "Girl... is... mine," Cal was reasonably sure the man wouldn't be getting up again.

He leaned down, found the pistol on Vorhoek's hip, and relieved him of it before hastening to Cat.

His gut clenched hard, and fear gnawed at him. The knife protruded from Cat's belly, but he didn't touch it; Cal may not have a lot of understanding of battle wounds, but he knew removing it may cause more problems, "Cat...." He ran an unsteady hand over her face, noting the pallor. "Don't leave me," he whispered. "I... I love you, dammit."

The hot tears that stung his eyes now fell unheeded as he swiped several strands of hair from her face. But her eyes remained closed, her breathing laboured.

The wail of sirens split the air, but he didn't look up, instead focussed on willing her survival. If he could, he'd give his life up for hers, well aware she'd already made that choice the moment she'd jumped from the car.

The selflessness of the action, ensuring they would be safely within the guarded building, wasn't lost on him at this time. But now, the reality was like a whiplash, sharp and stinging.

The sirens halted, and the sound of feet on the path intruded. He glanced up, and paramedics rushed toward him. "Over here. She's alive but badly hurt."

The racing medics pushed him aside, and he let them, though it was like carving his arms away. The need to stay warred with the responsibility for Sarah.

Helen appeared at his shoulder, her eyes shining with tears, her face pale. "Come inside. The ambassador and guards are on their way." She spoke slowly, softly, and he turned.

"She was willing to die for us."

Their gazes collided. "A brave woman. Do you think...?" Helen's words hung in the air.

He knew the question. "She'll live. I hope." But he wasn't sure even his bravado would be enough.

He waited at the hospital until he was given access to her bedside.

She lay so still in the bed, so pale, and he ached, whole body trembling still after six days of fear and little sleep.

Luisa joined him in the hall. "She's asleep."

"And?"

"I'm not supposed to tell you, but a medevac team will arrive in two days. If they're satisfied with her condition, she'll be repatriated to America. I can't hold her for you, Cal. You may be CIA, but whoever arranged her transport, they've got a private plane and a team arranged. Two doctors, nurses, and a supervisor." Her eyes were wide as if she'd never before seen this level of intervention in a medical transport.

"Dammit." He raked his hands through her hair. "I just need time with her."

Luisa smiled sadly. "And that I can't give you. You're not even supposed to be in here. It's only that your sister contacted me...."

Frustration, his constant friend, rose like a ravening beast in his chest. "Yeah. I know."

"You should go now, Cal. Before I get in trouble." Luisa looked over her shoulder to the doctor heading in her direction.

"You don't know anyone from the medical team?" He knew he had to leave, her concern blooming by the second as she shook her head. "If I get a note to you, can you make sure it travels with her? For when she's better?"

Luisa nodded. "Yeah, you know where to find me. Now go!" She pushed him forward and turned to greet the doctor.

Cal left, with great reluctance. He'd write down for Cat details on how to contact him, now that he was being recalled to America. He'd already been offered a placement in San Diego, not that he wanted it, but....

He shrugged. "What does it matter? At least I'll be on the same continent as her."

For now, that would have to be enough. Cal would work on the rest later.

NINETEEN

Tia didn't want to use the wheelchair they thrust on her. "I don't need it," she told Luisa, who shook her head.

"Hospital procedure. You're being released into the care of these nice doctors, but as we can't give you a clean bill of health, it's wheelchair or you stay longer."

That didn't appeal to Tia. The very fact that her knee had been replaced, the lack of energy, not to mention she still hurt—not that she divulged that to anyone—put her in a position where she couldn't argue.

"At least I might get good food in America," she growled, and Luisa laughed.

"Here are the packet instructions for the doctors, and the meds are ready for them to sign for in the dispensary. Plus, you'll need to sign some paperwork." Luisa thrust a clipboard at Tia, and she sighed, scrawled the well-practiced signature in her assumed name — the one she'd be using until they reached the airport. "What do you want to do about the flowers?" Luisa asked.

Biting her lip, Tia yearned to say, "I'll take them with me," but customs was tricky. "Give them to someone who doesn't have any visitors."

Luisa nodded and unclipped the folder. "Will do. Now, here are your copies, and I have something else for you." From the pocket of her duty clothes, she tugged out an envelope. White. No name.

She knew it was from Cal. Not that he'd been to see her. Tia blinked. "From Cal?" The words slipped out, no matter how hard she tried to hold them inside.

The nurse nodded.

"Where is he?" She'd resisted the urge to ask over the two days since he'd last visited.

"He had to fly home. He's been recalled." Luisa had already explained she knew Cal's sister in LA, having trained with her at the big private hospital with a trauma ward—a very well-known hospital that sprawled for several city blocks.

"Oh." She glanced away. "He didn't come to say goodbye." Why she felt so upset about that made zero sense; after all, by now, he'd be coming to terms with the fact that she'd done her job, they'd all survived, and he owed her nothing.

Unlike the way she felt.

Abandoned. Alone. Emotions Tia had never allowed herself to feel. It left her adrift.

"He tried. You were asleep. That's why he left this." She slid the paper into Tia's hand. "Now, security is here, so you can take delivery of your personal effects. The doctor and nurse on duty are expected in the next few minutes. Then you're out of here."

Strangely, taking control of her pack, rifle, pistols, and so on was emotionless. Like she was simply going through the motions.

By the time they were on the way to the airport, she felt like she was in an ocean and being buffeted by the swells... rushed into a future she wasn't so sure about anymore.

TWENTY

Tia suffered through the flight. The indignities of the constant checks, the stupid way they reclined her seat after take-off.

"I can take myself to the toilet," she muttered again.

The nurse rolled her eyes. "And we've told you more than once, no. If the plane banks suddenly or something, you'll fall. Then you'll have more surgery to look forward to. As it is, the doctors will want to tuck you safely into the hospital before you can go home. All things I've already told you."

"Nazi," she muttered.

"I heard that," the nurse quipped and disappeared. No doubt to formulate some new and unnecessary form of punishment for her to suffer through.

They were eating, she could smell it, but the only thing they gave her was mush. Wet sloppy stuff. "No chance of choking," the nurse offered with a smile. If Tia had been prone to tantrums, she'd have thrown the bowl back at the woman.

Just doing her job, whispered the angel on her shoulder.

Sucks, though, and the food is horrible, answered the devil.

Cal would have been making jokes, her brain offered.

He'd been recalled to America. It was good, she told herself. Entanglements in the business were dangerous.

If only she could make her heart believe that.

Tears stung her eyes, as they did regularly now. If only. Her battered heart found it hard to accept the truth. She felt strongly for the man. More so than she'd even done for Len. That had been a dalliance based on mutual affection, a demanding job, and few to no real connections.

With Cal, there was more. Deeper.

It was a difficult job, Tia. He left. Without a word, just a letter.

You were asleep, her brain reminded her.

If he'd wanted to see me, he'd have made an effort. Surely.

The hours of the long flight continued with her sleeping and grousing alternatively. By the time they touched down in San Diego, she was a mess—more so than when they'd taken off.

Once they landed, they wheeled in a chair, and strong arms lifted her before she could even attempt to rise. Using the food service lift, they manoeuvred her from the plane, swiftly completing the transfer to a gurney once they exited the small unit.

Cara waited inside the terminal for her. "Glad you made it," she said drily.

Tia simply grunted.

"Not feeling the love, huh? Anyway, now that you're back, we've made arrangements for your admittance to the private hospital, and even on release, we've got you a room at a rehab centre."

"I want to go home." She bit the words out, and Cara stared at her, gaze narrowing.

Tia bit her lip and looked away as she was wheeled to the waiting ambulance.

Cal entered his father's house. It hadn't changed, not really. But he had.

He'd left the envelope for Cat. His sister, who'd collected him from the airport, had taken him aside. "Luisa contacted me. She handed over the letter you left. Said Cat didn't say anything, just looked lost." Her gaze was full of questions.

The sort of questions he wasn't in any mood to answer.

He'd start the new job soon, a secondment that didn't appeal. He loved Santa Clarita, always had, but it wasn't home. Not that he had one. He'd move on to San Diego in a couple weeks, but for now, he'd lick his wounds.

"The kids are so happy you're home. When do you have to head off again?" Lisa's words slid through the veil of introspection.

He shrugged. "A couple weeks. I'm just waiting on some final information to come through."

They wouldn't ask many questions, more than a little aware that often there were things he couldn't say.

"Damien said to remind you that you owe him a game of racquetball," she offered, and he grunted, knowing damn well he was rotten company.

"And Dad wants to call a family meeting tomorrow night. I don't know what's going on, but he sounded pretty damn serious. He's been busy in the flower garden, pruning and weeding. Something big's going down, brother mine."

The flower garden. The one their mother had planted before she passed.

Had taken pride in.

He turned. "You don't know?"

Lisa shook her head. "Neither does Jo. All I know for certain is Dad wants to take us out to dinner tomorrow night, and he's got something he wants to say."

Was there a woman? A job? What could it be? But his natural inclination to question aloud melted away.

After all, until Cat contacted him, he felt like his life was in limbo.

Tᴵᴬ ʜᴀᴛᴇᴅ ᴛʜᴇ ʙᴇᴅ. Sʜᴇ ʜᴀᴛᴇᴅ ᴛʜᴇ ᴘʜʏsɪᴄᴀʟ ᴛʜᴇʀᴀᴘʏ, ᴀɴᴅ the food sucked. When Cara turned up on Wednesday morning, Tia was well and truly sunk in her frustrations. "Get me out of here, Cara."

The woman smiled and passed over the box of chocolates. "These are from Sarah, and Leonie says hurry up and get better. Her fill-in spotter sucks, according to her."

Tia grunted and shuffled in the seat. "I should be able to go home. They've got me on crutches and—"

"And you know why they aren't letting you home yet. There's no one to keep an eye on you, and that infection was pretty bad. They're only just sure it's under control. Your little sojourn to the vending machine and tearing the stitches didn't do you any favours, Tia."

All of which she knew, but it didn't make the situation any better. "I've got a request, Cara."

The woman settled into the chair opposite her. "What?"

"I need some youngsters found. In Zabuti."

Cara's brows rose, but she remained silent.

"Two kids. One is the son of Walter and Abidemi Umbarto. They think he's alive. I don't know, but he and his cousin were vocal against the militia. They were abducted. If they're still alive...." She dragged her fingers through shaggy hair. "Look, Walter and Abidemi arranged the transport across the border and into the national park. Details, as much as I can remember, are in my report." The one she'd given verbally from her hospital room just days after her arrival.

Cara set her mouth, eyes watching Tia's face as if questioning what had brought this request about. They rarely got involved in regional affairs. "I can certainly look into it, Tia. But you know it's not simple."

She was more than aware of that. The situation in Zabuti was still volatile, though the removal of Vorhoek, from what she'd heard via the team, was if not a mortal blow, then a serious loss.

The news had remained studiously silent about the Zabuti matter and the shooting of Tia, though. She told herself she was damned pleased about that.

"The Aussies and the US embassy should be able to help," Tia asserted.

"I'll put out feelers. Also, I've details on Sarah and Matthew Berding. He's been offered the ambassadorship but turned it down. Said the danger to his daughter was the reason. The kid's back at school, and her father has her in therapy. She's doing good, Tia. Your work was exemplary."

Tia blinked, feeling the sting of tears. "Good. I'm delighted. She's a good kid. She'll go a long way."

Cara's phone buzzed, and she answered, her eyes on Tia. "Yeah? Hmm? Okay, I'll be there soon." She reached out and touched Tia's arm. "I have to go, but I'll drop by again soon. Don't do anything I wouldn't," she added, and Tia laughed, the sound a little rusty.

"Well, there goes my wild orgy on the ward."

Cara grinned and rose, leaving Tia alone again.

TWENTY-ONE

Three Weeks Later

Tia waited for Sharon to arrive. She'd promised to come at two o'clock. Promptly. "She's probably lost in the world of code," she told herself.

So Tia waited, because Sarah was supposed to be her ride.

The hour of two came and went. By three o'clock, Tia was climbing the walls, more than ready after weeks to go home.

At three thirty, the door opened and in waltzed a contingent from the *Alathea Rangers*. Harmony, Stephanie, Cara, Leonie, and Sharon entered the room. If they were men, she might have thought herself drowning in testosterone. As it was, the estrogen was pretty damned overwhelming. In their matching uniforms of form-fitting jeans, shit-kicker boots, and figure-hugging T-shirts, they would capture more than one appreciative glance, she thought.

She pinned Sharon with a glare. "What took you so long?"

Sarah laughed. "I got busy, Tia. You know, sites to hack, bad guys to spy on. That kind of stuff."

Cara held out a bag. "Stuff your things in, and we'll get you out of here."

Tia took the bag and started shoving her clothes and toiletries inside. The book she'd read and her phone charger. "Why'd you all come?"

Leonie's face creased. "What, you don't want us here?"

Tia laughed. "You know that's not what I mean."

Stephanie shrugged. "Sexy doctors and interesting PTs do stuff for me, Tia."

Tia snorted. "You're in the wrong place, then. Not yet seen a good-looking doctor."

Not that she'd looked, because the image of Cal rose in her mind with a regularity she couldn't ignore.

The way his face creased in concern.

His smile.

But most of all, the way he'd branded her when he'd held her close and kissed her. Memories burned her day and night when she wasn't careful to keep them at bay.

"I've got news, Tia."

She stopped packing and pinned Cara with a searching look. "What?"

"Sharon and I've been busy. We found a way into the Zabutian militia records online. The kids you asked about?"

Tia's heart clenched. "What?"

"We found them," Sharon told her. "In a holding camp. They knew that if they disappeared long term, the repercussions would be wide-ranging. The Umbarto kid is a dual Zabuti/American citizen. He's got protection, and we've been able to push that with the embassy. The US troops stormed the holding camp two days ago. Both kids are alive. Safe."

The words hit Tia hard. She slumped into the chair, eyes burning.

"Tia?" Cara's hand came down softly on Tia's shoulder.

"I'll be fine, Cara. I just...." If only it were easy to explain the emotions swirling inside her. "I'll be fine," she reiterated.

"The kids are going to be offered therapy. They've seen bad shit, been involved in bad things, and it's going to take time to heal."

Tia nodded. "Yeah. That I understand."

Leonie cleared her throat. "Look, I know all the emotional shit is heavy, but I'd like to get out of here. Sooner rather than later, okay?"

Stephanie snickered. "Fucking wimp," she muttered, and Leonie laughed at the good-natured teasing.

"It's fucking good to be home," Tia growled, and they all laughed.

CAL CHECKED HIS PHONE, READY TO CONCEDE THAT PERHAPS CAT wasn't going to contact him. If she had, well, likely it would have taken place well before now. His mouth drooped as it usually did these days.

It was a bitter pill to swallow, he conceded.

For the first time in his life, he'd fallen for a woman—a strong independent type, to be sure, but one who was broken by her life experiences. The thing was his heart continued to tell him she was the only woman for him.

Except, even though he knew Luisa had passed along the note, she still hadn't contacted him. Could she not have felt the same connection between them?

The phone chirped, and he picked it up. "Hey, Lisa, how's it going?"

His sister was checking up on him. It seemed on his return, they'd decided it was the lot of his family to raise his flagging spirits. The CIA had nothing on his family when it came to committing to their task, he thought sourly.

"Nothing. I just wanted to remind you Dad has sold the house and is moving in three weeks. I know you can't get time off, but he wanted to know if there's anything you want. You were supposed to ring him on Friday... but you got busy?" The hopeful lilt in his sister's voice had Cal closing his eyes.

Days just seemed to blur since he'd been seconded to the governor's special task force. The CIA didn't usually do internal work for the state, but there were issues between one of the city councils and the state. It wasn't corruption, but someone was stonewalling on important decisions, so they'd decided to send someone in to "sniff out" what was going on. Rather like a special favour, according to his handler. The next six months would be long and arduous.

"Yeah, uh... nothing comes to mind," Cal murmured, well aware that his mom had only made the provision that her engagement ring should come to him. *I won't need it anytime soon.*

"I... I gotta go, Lisa. I'm attending an event tonight." Not that he was, but suddenly it was too much, and he just needed to let the silence surround him.

"Oh. Okay, then. If you change your mind, Dad'll need to know in the next week." He heard the concern in Lisa's voice, but he couldn't cope with more worry and disappointment right then. The loneliness and disappointment were beating him down.

He rang off after assuring her he'd check in the following evening, then looked out the window of the suburb where he'd leased a condo. The building was stark and somewhat ostentatious in the company of the older dwellings that also inhabited the street. This wouldn't have been his first option, except it was available and furnished when he needed it.

Cal sighed and retreated to the kitchen, opening the refrigerator door, then cursed. "Meant to collect some groceries." He'd been in a hurry to get home and had forgotten. Not that cooking was high on his priority list right now.

He considered ordering in, then shook his head. Better to stock up since he'd spun a line about going out to his sister.

He gathered up his billfold, keys, and cell and retreated to the garage. He could have ordered and had it delivered, but his mother's training stuck fast. He liked to choose his produce anyway. The drive wasn't long, and soon he found a spot and wandered into his favourite organic market. Once he had the cart, he moved slowly, choosing fresh fruits and vegetables, snacks, and drinks.

He'd almost finished when he looked up, his gaze drawn to a spot at the end of the row.

His heart nearly stopped, sputtering in recognition.

He knew that shape. That hair. The strength of those arms.

Cat. Moving slowly with crutches and precariously balancing a basket with pre-cooked meals.

The slow thud of his heart sped up, and without conscious thought, he moved. "Cat?"

She whirled, nearly toppled if he hadn't made a grab for her and pulled her close. "Cal? What are you doing here?" The breathless quality of her voice tugged at his heart.

"I'm shopping." He wanted to wince at the banality of his answer. "Oh, you mean here in San Diego? I'm on secondment to the governor's staff."

Lines bracketed her mouth. White marks that hadn't been there four weeks before.

"Here, let me take that." He reached out, taking the basket and placing it on top of his cart. "I'm not sure you should be carrying this. Should you?"

"I had to shop and get out of my apartment. It's.... The walls were closing in on me." She spoke quietly as if ashamed to explain the emotions that forced her to leave her home.

The weakness he understood, but the inability to accept it, he couldn't. Making a decision, he cleared his throat. "I'm done, how about you? How did you get here?"

She named a car service, and he grunted. "That's an expensive way to travel. I'll take you home."

Cat opened her mouth, then closed it, brow scrunching up. "I, uh... I won't say no."

He wondered just how bad her pain was.

They hurried through the register, and he indicated where he'd parked. "I can bring the car over—"

"No, I have to exercise it daily," she muttered.

Likely she was overdoing it, hoping to get back on track faster. Together they made their way to his car, a slow journey that on most days he'd curse. Today, he was grateful because providence had given him another chance—time with Cat.

Once they reached the car, he settled her inside. Then he stashed his and her shopping into the rear of the vehicle. "Where to?"

She gave her address, and he almost choked, given the complex she lived in was three doors from his own. The silence of the drive stretched, and the sky darkened as night stole its way across the earth. "Funny. It was much darker in Africa."

She turned to look at him. "I got your note."

His mouth twisted. "I know. Luisa is a friend of my sister's. It's how I got in to see you. You were supposed to not have any visitors. A security measure, I believe."

"Oh. That makes sense. I guess I wasn't in any fit state to question why you only came once or twice."

"Three times," he corrected.

"Oh. I mean...."

He took pity on her flustered appearance. "I wasn't able to stay long. My timing was poor, as the doctor was about to do his rounds. I came to tell you of my return to the US. You were busy, so I didn't stay. I tried again, but you were resting."

Her face flamed. "I was going to contact you. Soon. Once I was back on my feet. I got a report. Sarah's doing well. She'll be in counselling for some time, but she and her father flew out for Sydney the day after the incident."

Everything about the conversation was difficult and stilted. As if neither of them was sure what more to say. What they could discuss and what boundaries lay between them. Cal's chest ached, and it took all his willpower to stop himself from rubbing at his chest. Instead, he drove carefully, found her address, and parked.

"I'm on the ground floor. Better for me to come and go at all hours," Cat explained, and he gathered up her purchases and shadowed her to her door.

"Well," he said awkwardly.

"Thanks, Cal. For everything. I know it wasn't easy." She blinked as if she were also struggling for words.

"Yeah. Sure. Okay, well, I better be going." He retreated to the car but, once inside, sat there.

Fucking foolish.

He shook his head, thumped the steering wheel with both hands, then started the engine and drove until he found his designated spot outside his building.

TWENTY-TWO

Tia shook her head, making her way to the kitchen and dropping the frozen meals into the freezer. Long days and even longer nights were playing with her mind. "You're such a wimp, Tia. There was your chance to tell Cal you wanted to spend more time with him. Maybe have a relationship."

The truth was she didn't want to risk him turning away from her. It was better to be alone and not risk her heart.

But even as she turned away from the refrigerator, there, sitting on the kitchen bench, propped against her phone, was a reminder. The envelope she'd not been game to open since he'd left it for her at the hospital.

Her hands shook as she reached for it, broke the seal, and slid the sheet of paper from its confinement.

Cat, I know you're worried that what I feel will pass. On one level, I understand it would be easier for everyone if that were so. But it's not. What I feel is more than a fad or some kind of psychological connection forged in heat that will pass in time.

My feelings are real, Cat. I don't care that I don't even know your real name because I know the woman deep inside you. The one you hide from the world—the one with worth and who's afraid to be hurt again.

She's the woman I want to know better because I do care. I love you.

When you're ready, contact me.

Callum Gallagher.

He'd scrawled a cell number on the sheet too.

Tears welled, hot and overwhelming. "Oh God, what have I done?"

You turned away the man who claims to love you.

Suddenly a lifetime alone didn't seem like such a great plan. No one to snuggle with on cold nights. No one to return home to, to celebrate her victories with. No one was there in her corner when things got tough.

Oh, she had her sisters in the Alathea Rangers. Every one of them would celebrate if she called with good news. They'd commiserate too when things went wrong, but that wasn't the same. The idea of having one person intimately connected to you, unafraid to tell you what you needed to hear and wanting you as much as you wanted them....

Cara had recently found love, a man who'd stand by her side. If she could, why the hell couldn't Tia?

She reached for the phone, then moved back as if the receiver were a bundle of hot coals.

"I need a plan," she told herself. Because she'd already come so close to losing the opportunity, anything less than total preparation might spell the death knell of the hope that sprang forward now.

Deep down, Tia knew he did understand. At least, she hoped so.

She inhaled deeply, the seeds of a way forward echoing in her mind. "I need my sisters to carry this out," she whispered, even as she dialled her "sister" Harmony, who was affectionately known as

"Hell'" in the field, and calling to mind the blonde bombshell with hazel eyes and a penchant for speaking bluntly.

"Hey, Harmony. I need some help." Quickly, Tia explained the mess she'd made of things.

~

CAL'S CELL PINGED. JUST A TEXT. BETWEEN ONE MEETING AND the next, he was thankful he'd turned the sound back on so he heard it from across the room. They'd broken long enough to grab a coffee, and Cal took it as an omen.

He picked it up, and surprise filled him.

Hey, Cal. I should have rung you earlier. I kept the message you sent via Luisa. I just wasn't ready to read it until now. Can we meet? C.

His brain told him the message was from Cat. His hands shook, but he tapped back his response.

Sure. Where?

The three dots on the screen seemed to take forever to change to text, and he couldn't ignore the cold sweat that coated him while he waited.

Tia. My name is Tia. Meet me at Mission San Diego de Alcala? Say six o clock tonight?

He almost laughed, realizing she'd changed from military time to civilian, as she'd previously explained it.

Sure.

He cursed because, under normal circumstances, he'd just be leaving the office at six. "Not today," he told himself.

After that, the day dragged on and on, with pointless meetings and interviews. When he finally glanced at the clock, it was only nearly five. Concluding the meeting, he escaped to the office he'd been assigned and put his papers in order. Tonight was far too important, and he wanted whatever time it took to bring Cat—*Tia*, he corrected himself—round to his way of thinking.

Hustling for his car, he climbed inside it and peeled out, then swore again, caught in traffic. Every mile felt like it took an eternity, but finally he arrived at the mission site.

Sitting in the parking lot, he noted a blonde braced against a Maserati GranTurismo. The charcoal vehicle was crafted with a sleek front end and demanded he take a second look in the bay nearest the path to the entrance. Sleek. Dangerous. He wondered if that also described the driver.

Frowning, he glanced over and couldn't miss the way the woman seemed to watch him, her face serious, though he couldn't see her eyes behind the dark glasses. He had a feeling she was carefully summing him up and deciding if he was a danger to Tia. He guessed if she thought him to be, she'd have no hesitation in dealing with him.

He hustled up the path, and there by the front door waited Tia. A leaner version of the woman he knew.

"You made it." Her voice was soft but hoarse, as if she'd aggravated her throat.

"Yeah. You okay?"

Tia inclined her head. "Yeah. Umm, there's some seating over here." She lurched using the crutches. "I can't wait to get rid of these things," she snarled, and he smiled.

"Don't tell me. The doctor said if you take it slow, you'll recover more quickly?"

"Huh. You talk as much in riddles as he does."

They settled on their seats, and the silence stretched between them. Cal figured he'd give her time to think and tell him what she needed to say before he began his spiel.

"I should have contacted you before. I was afraid, Cal. I mean, all the books say those saved in those kinds of conditions feel hero worship for their protectors. That's not what I'm looking for."

"Neither am I, Tia." He reached out, taking her hand in his, savouring the strength of her grip. "You didn't come to save me. Your priority was Sarah. You told me often enough," he murmured, voice dry.

She laughed. "Yeah, I guess I did." She still hadn't turned to look at him, but the caress of her thumb over the knuckle of one finger was a tell in his mind.

"So, what next?" he asked, unsure what her answer would be but hoping for an agreement that there was a connection between them.

"I'm.... I don't know. I mean, I want to see if something can grow between us. I don't have a lot of experience in this area." Her cheeks pinked.

Taking a chance, he tugged his hand back, and as she gasped her dismay, he grabbed her chin in his fingers and turned her toward him. "Let's start with a kiss hello, then."

He kept the caress light and teasing, barely glancing flesh against flesh, but she didn't fight him. The whisper of her breath encouraged him, and the second time he moved in, there was unmistakable intent.

Lips opened beneath his enough to taste her essence as he ran his tongue along the soft, pliant flesh. She leaned in, and triumph roared primal and urgent.

"We need to talk, though, Cal," she whispered as she finally pulled away.

"About?"

"I come with lots of secrets and rules. My work...." Tia shrugged. "I love the work, and I love working with my team. But you have to know now"—she waved a hand over her leg—"it's dangerous. I'm gone for weeks on end, lots of times out of contact. I can't go into anything without you being aware, Cal. If that's a deal-breaker, tell me now."

He noted the tension that seeped into her frame and the white knuckles. What she was asking was... well, it was scary. She might one day go away on a mission and never return. Could he live with that? Did he want to live without her? Was he willing to accept that parts of her life would be kept from him? The idea of being without her, though.... "I don't like the thought of danger, but I can understand what you're saying. I've seen you in action and know you can handle yourself. I'm terrified when I think of the way you'd throw yourself on the line in the course of duty like you did for Sarah and me...." Just remembering dried his mouth and burrowed deep into his psyche. It would take time to come to terms with that, if he ever could.

She gave a nod. "Okay, then." She bit her lip, and her gaze scooted away. "I, umm...."

His brain acted like a frozen computer, and he searched for something to fill the sudden silence. "We should go out. On a date."

"A date?"

"Yeah. I would suggest dancing, but...." Cal indicated her knee, still encased in the cast.

"Huh. I have to rest it more, but hopefully within three months...."

Pleasure suffused him. "So, you're free for that long?"

"Until I get my medical clearance, I'm on office duties."

Laughter barked out of him. He could just imagine her sitting at a desk and answering phones, filing papers and reports.

The laughter died away. "So, where would you like to go for dinner?"

Her eyebrow quirked. "I'm not into fancy restaurants."

"Good. Neither am I. However, there's a mean pizzeria not too far from here in Little Italy. We could find a place near the beach to eat."

Her stomach grumbled, and this time they both laughed. "You've sold me on the idea. But I need to let Harmony know I'm going with you."

"The scary woman with the Maserati?"

"Oh yeah." Scooting forward, Tia rose, and he wondered at how effortlessly she seemed to do that with the crutches. "Come on."

He slowed his pace to keep time with her, and when she reached the other woman, he was surprised when Harmony removed her glasses. "So, got your rear into gear now, have you, Tia?" The tone was saucy as she scanned Cal.

He almost gulped when she turned to him. "Tia here may be dangerous, but I'm even more so. Hurt my friend and there won't be enough of you to bury, Callum Gallagher."

He blinked, aware that she knew his name and probably a lot more already besides that.

Tia sputtered. "Hey, you don't need to give him the 'big sister' chat, Hell. We're both adults."

Harmony shrugged. "Maybe, Tia, but you're weaker than me at the moment, so it's my job."

Tia rolled her eyes. "Thanks for the lift."

"You got it," answered Harmony as she rounded the car and flowed into the driver seat. The engine roared to life, but not before the window slid down. "Just remember, I know where you both live."

Cal helped Tia into the car, and she settled, nerves quivering from the awareness of the hot sexy man beside her. Even back in Africa, she'd been tempted, but with Sarah around, she'd fought it off. There was no Sarah now. And that feeling? It was there in spades.

It was just the two of them.

The car was quiet when he closed the door.

"So, where would you like to go?"

She bit her lip, glanced under her lashes at him. "We could... go to my place?"

He turned. "I'm not sure that's a great option. It could lead to...."

Moistening her lips, she plunged ahead. "I.... My home. Together."

"You're sure?"

She nodded. "Yes. We can order in or—"

"Later," he rasped, and her body responded, more than aware

that once they got home, sex was on the menu. God, her body was already burning, her inner muscles quivering just at the thought of it.

She laughed, unable to quell the sound.

He glanced at her. "What's so funny?"

"I was just thinking sex was on the menu, and then I realized we're both on it."

The glint in his eyes grew more dangerous. "Expand that theory for me, Tia."

She gulped. "How about just drive faster?"

CAL PULLED INTO THE DRIVEWAY AND RUSHED AROUND TO THE other side. The journey finished in silence with tension so palpable that cutting it would have taken a chainsaw. Now he opened the door, and she levered herself out, sliding crutches under her arms.

"Here, give me the key," he instructed.

She slid it out of her purse, handed it over, and made her way across the path while Cal zoomed-in, unlocked the door, and ushered her inside.

"Tia?"

"Yes, Cal?" Her voice was husky, and he moved from one foot to the other, standing in front of the door he'd just closed.

"I've... uh, it's been a while, and I don't—"

"Shhh, it's okay. After we set up the meeting, I grabbed some things." She opened her bag and showed him a drugstore pack. The outline of several boxes had him grinning. "I didn't know your preference, so I made sure to have a range."

His mouth dried. "I.... That's great, Tia." He squeezed his eyes shut because he wanted her so severely that he physically ached.

"Not changing your mind, are you?" She spoke so softly he had to work hard to hear her.

"No," Cal croaked, then jumped as the touch of her hand against his cheek surprised him.

"Cal?"

He sucked in a deep, unsteady breath and reached for her. "I don't want to hurt you or rush you, Tia. I mean, it's only been four weeks and...."

She grinned. "Maybe so, but with a bit of research online, I found a book on having sex after surgery. It's pretty good, and I've got a few ideas of my own."

He laughed, the woman's wittiness relieving the pressure. "Good. That's good. Great even. Now let's—"

"Shut up, Cal, and kiss me."

HER LIPS TINGLED AS THEY MOVED TOGETHER. CLOTHING melted by the bed after she'd led him to the room, then dispensed with the crutches once she half lay on the bed. "Cal?"

"You're... you're sure?"

He hovered, and she sighed. "You're not going to hurt me, and I'm a big girl. Unless you've changed your mind?"

He laughed. "Not likely." He crawled over the coverlet, clad only in socks and underwear, and she couldn't miss the outline of his erection.

"You could lose those," she muttered, and he laughed again.

"Maybe after you remove your bra and panties."

So Tia shimmied, hearing the twin movement of him disrobing. They came together, smooth but muscular naked skin glancing against a rough rigid torso, and she felt the electric arc of awareness.

Tia gasped and reached out.

"Careful," he murmured.

"Fuck careful," she retorted.

"Careful isn't here, and she's not the one I want to be with, but I don't want to hurt you or explode too soon," he answered on a laugh. Then he kissed her, rolling carefully, taking care to cushion her body before letting his hands roam.

Fingers found and caressed her breasts until her nipples tightened to hot points of lusty pleasure. They moved down her body, over her belly, which contracted against the slight touch, and found the thatch of hairs covering her centre. One finger slipped against her and then disappeared, sliding through the moisture that coated her entrance.

Mind-blowing. Heat and light. Fireworks.

She moaned and squirmed beneath him, all the while imploring, "Now, please."

He laughed, harsh with erotic hunger, then backed away as the climax loomed. Adrift in a sea of pleasure, he kissed Tia again, long and lingering, making sure to test every inch of exposed flesh. "Lift your leg, sweetheart," Cal whispered against her lips. With great care, he slid a pillow below the injured limb, and by the lamplight, he rocked back. "So damn beautiful."

If she'd been capable of words, now that he'd worked her to a frenzy, she might have bitten out a retort, but all she could do was reach out wordlessly. Her hand slid against his engorged cock, and he jerked with a whistle.

"Don't."

"Goose and gander," she muttered and continued her ministrations while his body hummed beneath her touch. Moisture dotted the slit of his head before she stopped. "Now, Cal. Fill me up. Love me."

"Condoms," he demanded, and she pointed to her bag, now forgotten on the floor.

"Shit!" He clambered from the bed, and it tossed and jerked as he scooped up the pack, retrieved a box, and broke the seal. Foil packets, in lines of three, slid to the floor while he cursed.

Cal grabbed one, ripped a single pack free, and retreated to the bed while his cock bobbed up and down, and that melted her insides a little more. Tearing at the pack with his teeth, he slipped the latex cover free and sheathed himself. "Last chance, Tia."

"Come to me."

He moved between her legs, nudged them open as his hands covered her breasts, and she gazed into his eyes.

"Now, Cal. Make us one."

He slid deep, and the wild rhythmic movements began, sliding and moving as the air sizzled between them. "I love you," she chanted, and he reciprocated with broken murmurings of love.

Deep inside her, the hunger and need grew, like a hot flame. It warmed her, urged her to meet each thrust and parry. It grew until there was no escaping, and finally, as her body held tight against his, Tia exploded in a wild orgasm that stole her breath and her senses.

In the middle of the night, Cal woke, his body rested in a way he'd long forgotten. A feeling of completion. Opening his eyes, it took a moment to orient himself. The warmth of a body beside him was reassuring.

Cat... no, Tia. Her name was Tia, and she was here. Beside him. Naked.

He lay there. His mind tossed over the question of whether this was only a short-term fling to satisfy the body's needs or the beginning of something more.

It could be either. Give it time.

His heart told him he wasn't after the short-term bang and boom. His brain said she'd warned him that the long term was problematic. But that was what he wanted. He just needed to make her aware that she wanted it too.

The morning after was always tricky. What to say, how to thank the guy. Usually her routine post-booty call was a cup of coffee, see them out, then retreat into her world. Head off to headquarters and hit the gym feeling limber and relaxed.

Today wasn't quite so simple because this was Cal.

"Do you...? Would you like a coffee?" *God, how much more inane can you sound, Tia?*

When Cal smiled, her insides turned to mush. "Sure. That'd be great."

She knew he watched her climb from the bed, and for the first time, she felt oddly awkward in her body. The instinct to cover her nakedness rising, she reached for her wrap.

"Umm, the shower's in there if you want one." She waved in the direction of the bathroom as she made her escape.

The coffee machine blinked with the bean compartment empty, and Tia cursed, reaching for the plastic container in the depths of the fridge and retrieving the scoop.

As she set about pulling out cups from the cupboard, her private cell rang—the number known only to the crew of Alathea Rangers.

"Tia."

"Not sure whether to say 'Good morning' or 'What's bitten you on the ass this morning,'" Cara's voice filtered down the line.

Tia groaned. "Hey, Cara."

"I have an update for you. Those kids from Zabuti? They were just the tip of the iceberg. The militia started singing after we sent in troops. They found about twenty more captives at other locations. They also found mass graves. They also picked up Harold Mubektu and Kezia Matcha. They'll both stand trial for their crimes, including the abduction of Sarah Berding."

Tia gripped the handset. "I hope they rot in jail," she muttered, looking at the doorway, aware that any second now, Cal would appear. "Is this...? What's the status of this intel?"

A long second passed. "Why? Something to do with the man Hell took you to last night?"

Hell knew who she'd met up with. Cal. That meant Cara did too. She cleared her throat. "Yeah, about that—"

"Tia, we're operatives, but that doesn't mean we can't have lives too. We can let that role consume us, or we can grow."

Tears welled in Tia's eyes. "Yeah."

Silence stretched. "I gotta go, Tia. I'll check in again later in the week, unless...?"

"No. That's fine. Thanks, Cara. For everything."

She'd only just slid the cell back to the benchtop when Cal appeared in the doorway. "Everything okay?"

She smiled. "Yeah, it's going to be good."

TWENTY-THREE

Five Months Later

Cal entered the condo, his step light. Tia had her final exam with the surgeon this morning, and he knew, if all went to plan, she'd be back on the roster. It was both a high and low in his mind. High because she'd be able to do what she loved and was good at. The low was the awareness of the danger she faced in her role.

"Hey, gorgeous!" he called as he dropped his backpack at the door, a habit they'd both taken up as a tangible reminder that work didn't intrude on their time together and entered the bedroom.

"I'll be out in a minute," she answered, and Cal heard her moving around in the bathroom beyond.

A proportion of their last five months had been spent on her rehabilitation. She'd chafed even as she'd undertaken a range of non-combat missions for the Alathea Rangers. It had given them both a chance to work on their physical stamina together, though. He'd used the time wisely, bulking up his regime in preparation.

They'd also been spending time together when their roles allowed for the first few months.

"This isn't working," he growled, rising from the bed.

Tia watched him, her gaze hooded. "Why not?"

"Because I'm sick of leaving you in the middle of the night, Tia. I want to be able to wake up in the morning and find you there, beside me. After a bad day, I want to come home to you and make a coffee or drink a glass of wine and know I don't have to leave until the next morning. You're not just a booty call." He shook his head. "This isn't how I foresee our relationship continuing." He indicated to the fact that he was half-dressed by moonlight.

Her sweet smile warmed him to the centre. "Hmm. Well, Callum Gallagher, what do you have in mind? Move some of your stuff here and some of mine to your place?"

He shook his head, knowing what he was about to suggest meant deepening what they already had. Cal settled on the side of the bed, taking her hand. "No, Tianah Warner. I'm suggesting we merge our lives. Live in one location. Together."

She stilled, her face taking on the arrested visage he knew meant she was weighing up his suggestion. "That's a big step, Cal."

"It is," he acknowledged.

"You've thought this out all the way?"

He nodded. "I have."

"Okay." Her tone was breathless, eyes sparkling, and he felt a lift in his chest at her answer.

"Good. So, how soon?"

"As soon as we can make it happen."

Cal had reached the end of his placement in the city manager's office, and he'd discovered that while he didn't enjoy the day-to-day managerial aspects of the role, for him, the real thrill lay in chasing down the culprit. A second-tier manager who'd been feathering their own nest, hoping for advancement by undermining and eventually removing his superior. Cal was pleased he'd been successful in finding the culprit.

His life, though, still needed to be realigned. The time had come to make decisions about his future.

He scratched his head because what came next might just rock both their worlds again.

Keeping secrets from Tia wasn't easy. Neither of the things he needed to speak to her about tonight was straightforward. The first thing? He wanted her to have her say before he committed. The second? It was the culmination of his dreams… six long months in the making.

Tia took a last look in the mirror, checking her appearance.

How she looked had never been a significant factor for her before Cal. She'd always washed it off, figuring if someone had an issue with how she looked, it wasn't her problem. Since him, that mindset had changed. She swiped her hands down the black leather pants and white peasant top she'd teamed with it.

A deep breath, and she opened the door to the great room. Leaning in, she kissed Cal on the mouth, feeling the ever-present burn of lust in her belly.

"You're home early," she whispered against his lips.

"All done. The office is packed up in the car. It didn't take as long as I expected. It's not like there was a party for my leaving. Once they realized the situation, I was the bad smell in the room."

She snuggled closer, inhaling his scent and glorying in it. "Come on. I've got dinner cooking and the table set in the courtyard. Just let me pour us a drink, and we can make ourselves comfortable."

Cal dragged off his suitcoat and tie, throwing them to the sofa, and for a second, Tia simply allowed herself to be swept away by his good looks and most excellent physique. One that had become even more toned since they'd started living together, now that he joined her for daily PT sessions.

He followed her to the kitchen and leaned back against the cabinets, the burn of his gaze setting off fireworks deep inside her.

The chardonnay lid unscrewed, Tia poured the wine, making herself think about the actions in the hope to quell the rising tide of desire, but her body refused to pay attention with everything stirring deep inside her belly.

When she turned and handed the glass, Cal took them both. "Tia? Come here." The deep hunger she'd been trying to ignore found its mate in Cal. He slid the glasses to the benchtop, then tugged her close. Their lips met, and the kiss could have melted the paint from the walls as he nipped and sucked. His hands found purchase on her hips and tugged her so close that she felt the planes of his chest, the power in his thighs, and the hunger too.

Sliding her hands to his shirt, she dragged it free and slipped her fingers across his broad back, relishing the heat.

When Cal tugged back, the red blush of arousal skated over his cheekbones. His eyes, well, they were pools of starvation.

"I... we...." Tia shook her head. "We should go out." She snatched for her glass. If the past were any indication, at this rate, they'd be in bed and dinner burning if she allowed the interlude to continue.

He laughed but followed her to the great room, and they settled into the deep padding of the sofa.

Sipping at the alcoholic drink, she observed him over the rim of her glass. "So, have you received another assignment yet?"

"I listened to your advice. I've taken leave for the next two weeks." He shifted in his seat, and she frowned.

"What? I mean, that's great, but—"

"I wanted to talk to you about... my future. I enjoy my work for the CIA, but it can take me anywhere." He shook his head. "Before we talk about that, your appointment? You got the go-ahead?"

He was hiding something. He'd tell her soon—she was sure, even though the knowledge was discomforting—so she nodded. "Yes, I'm good to return to active duty. Finally." The last six months of enforced rest, then rehabilitation would have been a trial if not for Cal. "I'm going to have to check in with Cara in the morning, though."

Cal nodded. "Okay, I can see that. I was thinking, though.... Your job takes you away a lot, but your base is here in San Diego. I rather like the sunshine, the beach, and being with you. I know we haven't talked about the future."

Her belly flip-flopped. "No, we haven't."

"I don't want to leave you, Tia. I love you." The words tumbled out, and the ache in her belly at the thought of him leaving, the one she'd tried to avoid, released just a bit. "You know that, and I need to consider if the CIA is the employer of choice for me now. This time, working in one location and coming home every night to you? It's been bliss. I don't want it to end."

Tia reached out, her hand finding him and holding on. "I don't want you to go either."

"I've made a decision. A company contacted me out of LA. They specialize in investigations dealing with political matters. It means I can live anywhere, so long as I have an office. I needed to talk to you first. I'd...." He cleared his throat. "If we continued this arrangement, we'd need a bigger place. A secure office for me, a training room. At least three bedrooms we could fit out."

Shock followed by elation filled Tia. She tempered them because he'd not been a front-line operative like she was. "And the dangers?"

"Not so many. I'd be researching. Though there may be times I'd have to travel, those trips would be minimal. Tia?" His gaze searched hers. "This is an opportunity for both of us. What do you think?"

No one had ever relied on her to make a life-changing decision like this. "Yes?"

Cal's frown was adorable. "Is that your answer or a question, sweetheart?"

Tia waited for a heartbeat, then grinned. "It's a yes, Callum Gallagher. I want you to stay and be part of my life."

His breath whooshed out, and even as she gathered herself, he held up a hand. "I have one more thing."

He fished around in his pocket. "In light of that, there's one last part of our relationship I want to formalize. Tianah Lee Warner, you are an amazing woman. Strong. Vibrant and unafraid to face challenges. Marry me. Let me love you for however many years we have together."

Shock slammed into her hard as he produced a small ring box, opened it wide so she could see the ring flashing in the light.

"I...." Trembling, she reached out. "I...."

Cal cleared his throat. "Is that a yes?" She didn't miss the quaver of concern in his voice and glanced up.

"It's a yes, Callum Gallagher."

With shaking hands, he drew the ring from the box and slid it onto her finger. "Good. Because no other answer would have been acceptable."

They kissed, the passion flaring brightly. Then Tia tugged away.

"Wait! What about dinner?" She moved her hand over his mouth so he wouldn't attempt to drug her again with that hungry caress that always seemed to undo her.

"It'll wait." His eyes glinted with pleasure.

"It'll burn," Tia answered, her gaze tracking to the kitchen and the meal sitting in the oven.

"Then we'll order in. Tonight is a time to celebrate." He grabbed her wrist, levered her up, and led her to the bedroom. The door clicked shut behind them.

***Did you enjoy this book by Imogene Nix?
There's more on the following pages. Just keep turning
to see what else.***

When Cupid—otherwise known as Diocail— is banished from his home on a remote Scottish Island, he's set a series of tasks by the great god Lugh, who also happens to be his father.

In **Blame The Wine**, he must bring two lovers together... BBW Cara and James, the man she's lusted over from afar who happens to be a super geek and head Veha Industries.

In **A Stranger's Embrace**, Diocail is driven to help an

emotionally fragile Jane and Davis, a famous author. The task is more complicated, with the existence of Carstairs her could-be ex-husband and teenage daughter, Frannie.

In **Revenge on Cupid**, Diocail must take the ultimate chance and find his own happily ever after with Simone. Sometimes the past gets in the way and HEA's don't come cheap though.

The dusty, dingy little diner was full, even with its current state of cleanliness—or lack thereof. People from the surrounding offices didn't care about anything except the incredible, well-prepared food at a reasonable cost. They flooded in, like waves to the shore. As one tide left, another swept in.

"Honestly, Simone. I'm going to try getting his attention one more time. If that doesn't work, I'm out of there. I mean, how long can I keep trying?" Cara picked at the caramel tart she hadn't been able to resist with the cheap metal fork and flicked the blob of fresh cream that sat on top to the side of the plate.

"You've said that tons of times before. Besides, what are you going to do to get his attention? Hmm? Walk naked through the typing pool?" Simone bobbed the straw in her smoothie as she eyed her friend with a frown. "It's been what? Eighteen months since you saw him, and you've mooned over him from a distance ever since you met him. You need to move on, Cara. That is, unless there's something you haven't shared?"

The query was arch. Cara shivered even as she shook her head. "No."

Simone quirked an eyebrow, obviously unconvinced with the answer. Cara let out a deep sigh of frustration. "There's a position...it's only temporary, for a PA reporting directly to him." She speared a forkful of tart, chewed quickly and swallowed, before continuing. "In his office, full-time for the period of the engagement. I saw the memo yesterday. I mean, I have the skills, right? I can type, answer phones, make coffee, file, greet people. What's more, I can probably do it better than all those size eights in the typing pool that

Ms. Jackman seems to prefer." She nodded thoughtfully. "All I have to do is get past the ogre in Human Resources."

Simone stared at her, disbelief clear on her face. "Girl, I so remember that woman. If you think you can get past her, you're doing better than I ever did. That's why I left Veha Industries, remember? Maybe it's time to haul out your resumé and consider some other options. Look for something better." Simone shook her head and billows of her crimson hair swirled through the still air.

Cara understood Simone only had her best interests at heart. But this time she knew the outcome would be different. Hell, she could feel it in the air. The tingle of expectation.

"Cara, the HR ogre will hang you out for breakfast before she offers you anything like a position in that office. Remember her mantra? Good looks and good work make for a positive workplace!"

Simone didn't sugar-coat anything. It was another great reason for their long- term friendship. Honesty. But Cara didn't want to hear the truth in the statement. Even if it was exactly as her friend said.

Cara nodded quickly. "Yeah, I know, but if I don't try, then I won't know how close I can get to him, right? And the only way to catch his attention is to get past *her* and see him in person." Cara quaked a little at the information she needed to share. The favor she needed to ask. "Anyway, I tidied up my resumé and dropped the application into a memo envelope yesterday, so it's too late to back out now. I mean, fortune favors the brave. Doesn't it? If I don't snag an interview, I'm going to visit the career advisor across the street and register with them." She shrugged. "I'll look for temp work until something more long-term shows up. I can see what they have on offer and well...who knows? Maybe a job with the right boss is just waiting for me. But I'd rather this worked out, to be honest." Her voice trailed off into a whisper. "I really wish he would notice me."

Simone took a long slurp of her banana drink, and Cara noticed her questioning gaze even as she squirmed. Finally, Simone nodded. "It's your funeral. So anyway, you'd better show me this memo if you want me to be a referee for you. I'm guessing that's what you need, right? I'll have to know what I'm supposed to say about you before they ring."

Cara smiled. "Thanks, Simone. I knew I could count on you." She slipped a piece of paper out of her handbag and handed it over. "Sorry it's a bit creased. It was in the bottom of my bag, I stashed it so none of the others from the pool would see. You know how it is."

Available from Love Books Publishing
books2read.com/CelticCupid

Direct Autographed Copy
https://www.imogenenix.net/CelticCupid

STAR OF ISHTAR

Warriors of the Elector
Book One

The first time Elara laid eyes on Grayson was when he rescued her from the clutches of a madman and his scientists who were kidnapping humans and conducting horrific experiments on them. That was years ago. In spite of her attempts to deepen their relationship, they remained nothing more than close friends. Now Elara is a medic with the Admiralty, and she knows what she wants. It's been Grayson since the beginning. When Elara is stationed on the *Star of Ishtar*, she arrives with a plan to further her career. But this time her plan has an added bonus—to finally get her man.

Grayson's spent years fighting the connection between himself and Elara. He's certain it only exist because he saved her life. But his will is failing, and he fears he just might give in to temptation.

"I finally made it." Elara Sudonne watched as the hull of the *Star of Ishtar* loomed in the inky darkness. She clutched her hands tightly together as the shuttle approached the hulking battleship.

This would be her new home and first combat ST placement for the Earth Empire. She quaked inwardly with nerves but fought to keep her serene exterior. Previously her deployments had consisted solely of on-planet expeditions and in rehabilitation and dirtside facilities. When the chance had arisen to move to the battleship, she'd grabbed it with both hands.

The frigid air chilled her bones as she sat in her shuttle seat, but a trickle of sweat inched its way down her back under the fresh gray wool flight uniform. Little puffs of vapor escaped her mouth as she rubbed her arms. Nerves stretched tight, she looked through the small portal at the front of the vessel. She wanted to tug at the collar that somehow seemed to have grown tighter as the ship loomed ahead, but instead she firmed her mouth, straightened her spine, and concentrated on the future.

"So damned long." She'd been working toward this outcome since the day Grayson Myatt and Duvall McCord had saved her from her Ru'Edan captors. She was lucky, she'd survived the 'experimentation' of the Ru'Edan leader Crick Sur Banden's scientists. "And all I have to remind me are my scars." She didn't grin at her own joke.

The person seated behind her jostled but she ignored it, lost in her memories. On that day, so very long ago, the young Elara, fresh-faced and with idealistic views of the empire, was taken from the mall where she'd been shopping with friends, thrust into the back of a transport vehicle, and given to the Ru'Edan scientists to experiment on.

For days they'd worked on her and others, seeking an average pain threshold of humans, slicing her skin then noting reactions and how long it took to heal. They'd cut her arms, body, and even her face, and now she carried the extensive scarring of the exercise as a reminder to herself and others of what they were fighting for. Freedom. The freedom of Earth and its allied planets.

She'd never relinquished hope, it had been her constant companion as she fought against the all-consuming terror. Then they'd found her in that dirty, disused warehouse. They'd found others too, in various states of death and decay. The smells of despair had filled the air with a fetid ripeness that she'd never been able to forget.

Since that day she'd promised herself that she would pay the Ru'Edan back for what they'd done to her. What they'd taken from her. Over the years, she tempered and honed the rage while remaining adamant that she would see the final act played out. She couldn't physically fight, but she had learned about trauma, knew it and understood how it affected a person, and used it as a weapon.

The iron will forged through her experiences had fed her determination, and she'd applied herself to study, finishing in the top ten percent of her class. She entered the medical program at the academy, working hard to excel. Her family remained supportive if perplexed as to why she had chosen to keep reminding herself of what had happened.

The maw of the *Star of Ishtar* loomed closer, opening its cavernous mouth as she watched through the portal. She could hear the voices of the shuttle crew signaling their intention to enter and land, the tinny confirmation coming swiftly. She watched avidly while the shuttle maneuvered, imagining the invisible shields dropping to allow it entry.

Her hands twisted with fear and anger, but she tamped down her emotions. Anger never helped anyone. Staying strong, knowing your history, and ensuring it couldn't be repeated, they were the answers, she told herself firmly, pulling herself from the grip of a dark past so horrific she still saw it in her dreams. She pushed it away to the recesses of her mind and focused on what she was about to do.

A squark overhead, the usual mechanical sound that alerted all on board to a transmission by the captain, caught her attention. "Attention all passengers. We are entering the shuttle bay. Please ensure when you disembark you remove all personal items. Move beyond the white line and wait for your designation."

The lights of the bay flashed as they entered, and once again Elara marveled at how far humanity had moved since they had first walked the Earth. She saw the opening of the structure as the shuttle moved into the bay, inching forward slowly until it stopped its ponderous motion and began its descent to the floor. Something deep inside warmed even as the shuttle's environmental systems began to synchronize with the cooler temperature of the *Star of Ishtar*, and she felt a smile crawl its way over her face.

Elara breathed in deeply, inhaling the metallic-tasting, recycled air and welcoming the calmness that settled on her body. Her eyes closed as she filled her lungs. "I'm here." There was more than a little satisfaction in her tone, and she smiled. She slowly exhaled, finding that center of peace she relied on.

A loud thud and clank echoed as the deep drone split the air. The engines were powering down, and there she was, on one of the Earth Empire's Emeritus class battleships. She sat in her seat, waiting for the all clear from the captain, and once it sounded through the cabin, she rose, tugging at the webbing belt and disengaging it.

The small backpack beside her was all she carried as she made her way to the exit, not needing to duck as so many others did. She stepped through the door, her hands gripping the rail of the cold, metal stairs which connected to the side of the gray shuttle.

She clambered down them slowly, savoring the experience. The sting of the cold on her hands from the stairs, frigid from even their brief exposure to the blackness of space, made her flinch inwardly. The shuttle journey from the Admiralty's strategic base at Aenna to their current position had taken just over an hour, but the whole time it felt like her heart had been in her throat. Her mouth was dry as she followed the new recruits from the ship into the landing bay. She stopped, silently noting the slight mustiness of the air, the recycled quality easily recognizable. Everything, including the oxygen, needed recycling in space.

All around her people swarmed, either around the ships or into the dogleg line that now formed ahead of her. Someone had opened the baggage locker of the shuttle, and the sound of dropping bags hitting the plascrete floor echoed in the air. Another crewmember guided trolleys to the other side of the shuttle, pulling out boxes with important day-to-day items for the ship, including vaccines and plants. She watched briefly, all the while listening to the alien cacophony. Voices called in welcome to old crewmembers, while new ones watched, many goggle-eyed in the fresh uniforms of newly minted officers and crewmembers.

Her gaze flicked around quickly, taking in the sights, sounds, and smells, pungent with oils and grease; burning smells from the scorched plascrete and the press of sweaty or nervous bodies. She joined the line silently, tacking onto the end, and stayed at parade rest, knowing the welcoming voice would cut through the air soon enough. She felt somehow disconnected from the main throng. Perhaps the knowledge that this was the outcome she had worked for years to achieve set her apart. However, still, she felt so...distant from everything around her. She smiled secretly at the bout of whimsy.

"Attention!" The voice boomed out over the plascrete of the docking bay, and she snapped her body into position, noting the commander who had bellowed the words. Technically, she outranked most members aboard the *Star of Ishtar*, except for the command and leadership staff, but she knew all newcomers had to join the welcoming parade, regardless of rank.

Fleet Captain Elphin came into view, his tired features topped by salt-and-pepper gray hair, which highlighted his cool blue eyes. Elara also recognized a body prone to a little middle-aged thickness. Following behind him was his second-in-command, Duvall McCord. A young up-and-coming officer, his status as a fast-tracking officer heading toward his own command, with Elphin both his mentor and captain, had become almost legendary at the academy.

She looked closely at McCord, noting the dynamic drive of his actions and movements. Soon he would achieve a promotion to captain, and she rejoiced for her friend. She'd followed his career with interest and had to tamp down a smile as his eyes betrayed the shock of seeing her before settling into their flat command persona. So he hadn't been apprised of her deployment, she noted, and she had to restrain the tiny feeling of surprise and satisfaction. She filed that snippet of information away.

She caught sight of the man standing behind Duvall. Grayson Myatt. He'd made her heart beat faster for years. Tall and blond with a muscular build and a sexy, tight, little butt, he had pools of deep-blue eyes that had always made her think of forever. He had a growth of stubble on his chiseled jaw, and her fingers itched to touch his perfect lips. Yes, since the day he'd found her in that nasty warehouse tied down like a ragged animal, she'd worshipped him from afar.

Now she had her opportunity to tangle with him, hopefully much closer than any chance that had ever come her way before. With a sigh, she pulled her gaze back to the captain and forced herself to concentrate on his words. She couldn't afford to have her commanding officer angry due to her being distracted.

"Welcome to the *Star of Ishtar*. Most academy recruits want to join us because of what we represent, but on this ship, we only take the best of the best. So, if you made it here, you're the ones we wanted to take a look at. Getting here is only the first step. Staying here is harder to achieve. Our people are the best. Earn your place, and in return, we'll make you one of our crew—a member of the *Star of Ishtar*. Only the best and the brightest wear our uniform and badge. You'll be expected to perform to your absolute limit then give some more. We don't tolerate people who don't pull their weight. Do us proud and wear your uniform with pride." The captain looked out over the new members of his crew. His voice had echoed during his speech, and now it died away.

He scanned the faces before him, and she could almost read his thoughts. There were new security officers and a smattering of other crew. Some of them were young and impressionable, and she knew a few wouldn't make the cut as crewmembers. Others would carve out their place on the *Star of Ishtar* and move to better positions and placements, like she would: the new SurgiTech, a younger female, experienced but untried on board a ship. She smiled at that thought.

Some of those who stood with her would be replaced as they failed the exacting standards the captain set. She'd heard that he was a firm captain, fair but demanding. He'd have to be to command this ship. The Ishtar had well over five hundred at full capacity, and the captain could select their placements as his command staff saw fit from the many who applied to join the crew. She sensed his satisfaction with the choices in the relaxation of his body.

Abruptly, he turned to Duvall, breaking her study of him. "Get them to where they need to present themselves." His words echoed as he walked away. He had a purposeful stride. Quick but unhurried, like he knew where he was going and how to get there. A man who knew how to get what he wanted. Someone to respect and admire.

"My name is Commander Duvall McCord. I am your second-in-command, and my direct subordinate is Commander Grayson Myatt. While you are aboard the *Star of Ishtar* you will be required to fulfill your duties efficiently. As Captain Elphin said, do your job right and you will be one of ours, with all the benefits that come with being a crewmember of the *Star of Ishtar*."

He paused and eyeballed each of the newer recruits, those fresh from the academy. Many of them paled under his gaze, and she smiled inwardly. Even the older people in the line seemed to quake beneath his scowl. He'd always had that air of innate authority, even when barely out of the academy himself. She knew his methods and watched him make full use of the carefully practiced tone of presence.

"Each of you has been assigned. You will present yourselves to the chief of your section. Those details will be found in your orders. Commander Myatt has organized a team to escort you to your cabins. You will have approximately one hour to prepare. We've arranged for crewmembers to escort you to your superiors. Be ready to present for duty. Any issues, you will, of course, take up with your section commander. Should there be need to take any further action, you will see Commander Myatt. You should only see me if you are a command crewmember or as a point of discipline. I am not one for small talk, so if you present to me, have a very good reason."

He delivered the words slowly and deliberately, and Elara restrained a small smile on hearing at least one gulp from those in the line nearest her.

"We run a tight ship here. Discipline and commitment are the two key factors we look for beyond loyalty in our crew. You will from henceforth represent our ship everywhere, and we do not tolerate anything less than the best." He looked around once more, the stern demeanor he wore so well reinforcing the message. If she hadn't known him for so long, she too might have missed the hint of humor glinting in his eyes, the one many took for coldness.

Her legs ached, and she wanted to move and relieve the pressure on them, but she held herself still, waiting for the command to dismiss. She wouldn't let herself or him down now. Not after she'd worked so long to achieve this position.

As the new ST, she had no previous experience on ships. She had vast experience in the field, but Elara was aware that would count for little in the eyes of most of the crew. She didn't intend to signal a weakness to anyone and least of all on her first day aboard the *Star of Ishtar*. That thought held her still and controlled.

She had big shoes to fill after her predecessor, Jamieson, had retired, even though she knew she could fill the void he'd left behind. As a long-term member of the crew—over twenty years—his tenure on the *Star of Ishtar* had placed him aboard since its launch. Due to his experience in the heat of battle with the Ru'Edan he had made a name for himself as the coldest of cold in the hottest of situations. She hoped to emulate that herself and carve out her own place aboard the Ishtar, as its crew lovingly knew her.

Duvall and Grayson knew how much she wanted to prove herself. They just wouldn't have expected it here, on the Ishtar.

She watched Duvall study her, then, quickly turning on his heel, call to those assembled, "Dismissed."

Once they started to move away, she softened her stance, preparing to turn when the call came.

"Sudonne! A moment if you please."

Elara turned to face Duvall. "Commander?"

"Welcome to the *Star of Ishtar*, Elara. While I am surprised you're the new ST, Grayson and I are pleased you could join us. But how did you manage to pull it off? Keeping it quiet that you were the new ST?" he asked, his voice deep enough to make most women shiver with anticipation.

She smiled, thinking it was a shame she didn't have any feelings for him except sisterly attachment, but then again, given his lack of deep commitment to women, maybe it wasn't such a shame after all.

She understood what drove him. He wanted his own ship and to captain his own future. They'd spent many nights over wine or ale discussing his beliefs that commitment grounded a person. Inwardly, she shrugged. He'd make those calls for himself, though she was sure that one day he would come across someone who would make him consider his choices a little more thoroughly.

"I'm pleased to be here, Duvall. Having an uncle who happens to be an admiral, he was able to let Captain Elphin know that I wanted to surprise you. It's a small world in the Admiralty. Elphin already knew of me, so he okayed my placement. Once the powers knew there was no impediments to me joining the crew, it was fairly simple from there." She felt a small smile creep onto her face, then let it drop away. "What do you think Grayson thinks?"

"Ah, still chasing him, are you?" He grinned, his eyes twinkling. "I think he'll be pleased you're finally old enough and you're here." He looked her straight in the eye. "But you may just need to remind him of that particular fact." He motioned for her to go before him, barking out a deep laugh. "Come on, I'll show you to your cabin."

Available from Love Books Publishing
Available in Ebook via Books2Read

Direct Autographed Copy
https://www.imogenenix.net/Warriors1

THE BLOOD BRIDE BY IMOGENE NIX

Hope just wants to be an ordinary nestling. She went to college and escaped, but now she's back and there's a secret everyone is keeping from her.

Xavier is the new master of the nest, ready to welcome home the daughter of the house who he has never met. He's unprepared for the woman who steals his breath and enchants him.

Now Hope and Xavier must fight for lives and those of the inno-

cents. After all, it is only by overcoming the rogues that they will have a chance of a timeless future together. But will it be in time?

PROLOGUE

As silence descended on the house, the shadows grew—dark grays and blacks that bled into each other. First one figure then another broke away, making a run toward the house. Silent as the grave, they moved swiftly over dew-slicked grass. Then they stopped still. Waiting. Not a movement betrayed them until a signal propelled them back into action and they started crawling upwards. The walls damp coating no barrier to the intruders that ascended in the darkness.

The sound of each window breaking shattered the quiet—the figures were inside. Screams echoed through the night. Yet, in this area of large estates, heavy with noise-absorbing shrubbery, no one could hear those within. The blood-curdling screams went on and on before finally dying away.

Just one sound echoed through the night: The sobbing of a child.

The front door opened and figures trooped out—ghostly specters against an inky night sky, broken by a single outline. A child in white, carried at the center of the pack.

No sound broke the silence as they moved toward the trees surrounded the house.

Flames now licked at the manor: A deathly glow of oily smoke rising.

All that remained was a single person—wrapped in a cape of midnight blue beyond the house—watching them melt away.

Jemima moved toward the burning structure, breaking into a run as she breached the threshold. Vainly she attempted to enter, but the heat drove her back.

Now dashing tears from her face, she raced across the graveled driveway toward the gates, where the guardhouse was located. No sign of life existed within the building and some instinct of survival slowed her pace to a careful creep. Out of breath and heaving from exertion, she nervously checked within.

Small puffs of white vapor colored the glass. She darted from one window to another. Her cloak drawn tightly around her body, hoping it would camouflage her from sight.

Satisfied, Jemima entered through the heavy, wooden front door and moved toward the phone she spied on the floor. Her eyes darting here and there she dialed, listening to the rotary motor as it returned to the proper position. Time was short and if *they* came back, she needed to have shared the message.

The phone rang once. Twice. With a brrping sound it connected.

"Hello?" A male answered and she felt a warm flush of relief at the voice. A voice she knew well.

"The manor has been breached. The girl child taken." The words erupted and her hand trembled.

"On our way." The click of the receiver being replaced echoed loudly in the stillness of the room.

Copper. She smelled copper.

Her stomach soured, knowing it meant more deaths. Jemima looked around for the gun—a gun with deadly, holy water-infused copper bullets—she knew was hidden somewhere in the room. A gun she couldn't find. *No divine intervention exists here*, she thought.

Hopefully *they* didn't remain. Feeding. If they were still here, that's what they would be doing. She found a corner and scrunched down, hiding from sight.

Crouched low, she tried to stay as still as possible, listening for sounds of the vehicles she knew would be coming. She dug her fingers into the flesh of her arms; remaining aware enough to stop before drawing blood. That would surely bring them out. Jemima dragged the cloak around her to capture the warmth, yet there was little to be found.

The sounds of engines roused her from the corner of the room. Jemima inched toward the window, the lead of the old glass distorting her view, hearing raised voices she knew Mistress Cressida had arrived.

Jemima retreated. Remained hidden from the woman because if she knew, all may well be lost. From the shadowed room she listened to the conversation...

"It smells like Estersham." The Mistress' eyes closed. "If it is, we have a problem." She turned once more, her face set and eyes now glacial in intensity. "James?"

The man nodded as if he knew what was to come.

"If I take those steps, I cannot return. Another must stand in my place." Her voice hardened while her eyes glittered in the dim light, piercing in their intensity.

Then the Mistress' voice called out in the near silence. "You and yours have been my loyal servants for so many years. I took an oath to protect you long ago. I renewed it with marriage and births, over and over. Now, my home and yours have been breached and this child taken from us. The girl child, who will be the hope and salvation of our kind, was ripped from the bosom of our nest. I will repay your loyalty and I will get her back." The words of power rippled in the night and licked at Jemima's skin.

Available in Ebook
books2read.com/BloodBride-Nix

Direct Autographed Copy
https://www.imogenenix.net/BloodBride

ALSO BY IMOGENE NIX

<u>Warriors of the Elector</u>

- Star of Ishtar
- Starline
- Starfire
- Star of the Fleet
- Starburst
- The Star of Eternity

The Star of Ishtar & Starline - Print

Starfire & Star of the Fleet - Print

Starburst & The Star of Eternity - Print

<u>The Secrets World:</u>

<u>Blood Secrets</u>

- The Blood Bride
- The Illuminated Witch
- The Sorcerer's Touch

<u>House Secrets</u>

- As Dawn Breaks
- Immortal Consequences
- Unnamed Book III

All That Glitters - a House Secrets Novella (Coming in 2023)

<u>Danu's Secrets</u>

- The Downfall of Padraic O'Shaunessy (Coming in 2023)
- Unnamed Secrets Book II

The Automaton Series

- Haven House (Coming 2022)
- Nobel Crest (Coming 2022)

The Search Duology

- Miss Elspeth's Desire
- Miss Isabelle's Craving

Reunion Trilogy

- War's End
- The Assassin
- Executing Justice

The Reunion Trilogy in Paperback

Sex Love & Aliens

- Tangled Webs
- False Webs
- Covert Webs

21st Testing Protocol

- Cyborg: Redux
- Children Of A Greater Evil
- When Evil Came To Stay
- Finis: The War To End All Wars

Celtic Cupid Trilogy

- Blame The Wine
- A Stranger's Embrace
- Revenge On Cupid

The Celtic Cupid Trilogy in Paperback

<u>Zombieology</u>

- The Reset
- I Dream of Zombies
- The Six Million Dollar Zombie
- Make Room For Zombies (2022)
- Unnamed Zombiology Book (coming 2023)

<u>Knights of Pleasure</u>

- Silken Knights (Coming in September 2022)

<u>Single Titles</u>

The Chocolate Affair (also in Print)

Falling In Love Again (Previously A Sapphire For Karina)

BioCybe (also in Print)

Hesparia's Tears (also in Print)

Tomorrow's Promise

A Bar In Paris (also in Print)

Inheritance Of The Blood (also in Print)

The Plan

Loving Memories (also in Print)

Hero of Heartbreak Hill (also in Print)

My One & Only

Curse Bound (coming 2021)

Raspberry Dreams (Not Yet Released)

Non Fiction

Self Publishing: Absolute Beginners Guide (With Suzi Love)

Written as Ciara Cave

25 Curated Ways To Get Rid Of Telemarketers

Book Signings for Absolute Beginners

ABOUT THE AUTHOR

Imogene is published in a range of romance genres including Paranormal, Science Fiction and Contemporary. She is mainly published in the UK and USA.

In 2010, Imogene Nix (the pen name not Imogene herself) was born. Imogene sat down and worked tirelessly for 3 months culminating in the book Starline, which became the first in a trilogy titled, "Warriors of the Elector." Since then she's had over 30 titles published and is now focusing on hybridising herself - with a mixture of traditionally published and self published works.

In fact, she's taking control of many of her back catalogue books, which are slowly re-releasing as self-published titles.

Imogene is a member of a range of professional organisations world wide, and believes in the mantra of mentoring and paying it forward and is actively involved in mentorship (through NaNoWrimo and her vlog: In The Chair With Imogene Nix) and tutoring of new and upcoming authors.

In her spare time she loves to drink coffee, wine & eat chocolate and is parenting more than one spoilt cat along with her husband and daughters and looks forward to weekends away with her husband in their caravan "The Seven Year Hitch!" Do look forward to her caravan romance at some point!

To Contact Imogene

www.imogenenix.net
imogene@imogenenix.net

facebook.com/ImogeneNix
twitter.com/ImogeneNix
instagram.com/ImogeneNix
bookbub.com/authors/imogenenix